# CASTILIANO VULGO

A work of historical fiction, in two languages,
devised purely from an Elizabethan dictionary
as found online while researching the great
Elizabethan times.

# TABLE OF CONTENTS

Part 2 written in modern English terminology

1.

2.

3.

4.

5.

6.

7.

8.

9.

10.

11.

12.

13.

Part 3 is written in both languages

1.

2.

3.

4.

5.

6.

7.

8.

9.

10.

11.

12.

13.

# Introduction

1603, London, England

Dr John Dee returned to England several years before and continued his work without Edward Kelley, he was awarded a position in Manchester but it isn't long before he returns to Mortlake.

Gradually, it becomes clear that he needs another assistant besides his eldest daughter, Katherine. After severely having his fingers burnt with Kelley's tricks, and two fake scryers in the form of Bartholomew and Heckman, he's dubious of everyone coming forward for the post.

He overhears Hendrick and his drunk companions talking in the local ale house, and Hendrick is defending Dee's genius. Hendrick is severely injured in a fight where he is stabbed in the face leaving him blind in one eye and with a permanent facial disfigurement. But even that isn't enough to dissuade him from the work with Dr Dee when it is offered to him by the man himself.

Hendrick is overawed to be offered the prestigious role of his assistant. He is awestruck by Dee's laboratory, offered lodgings with the Dee family and introduced – agreeing a pact that his position must remain secret in order to protect the delicate work involved.

The more time Hendrick spends with them, the more he appreciates Dr Dee's genius – and he falls in love with Katherine, who rejects his advances at first but is gradually worn down.

Although this story is a work of some historical fiction, there are facts that have been interwoven in order to educate and entertain the audience. We hope you enjoy the two part tale, unusually written in Olde Elizabethan language and then converted into more familiar modern terminology.

There is also a third part with both together that shows how the tale was woven, for those who are curious!

## Note from the Author

Having performed research for a project several years ago containing Elizabethan, I fell in love with the language and wondered if I could write a tale using it.

Naturally, writing in two languages is difficult: but now, three years into the making, I'm pleased to publish this work to coincide with the 400th anniversary of William Shakespeare's birth. The eagle eyed amongst you will see he has a cameo in this tale.

Please note that this is not in my usual writing style; the chapters do not flow seamlessly. I hope that the format entertains and amuses my readers – that is my chief aim after all – and I have woven some historical facts into the work as well.

I hope you enjoy the book.

Yvonne

## Part 1 written in Elizabethan language

# 1.

Outside, the ward watchman strode by, walking his route up to the port and back again.

The foister, the nipper and their shadows skirted the pools of dark, biding their time.

Hendrick looked around, seeing faces that he didn't recognise and some that he did, realising that most of the drinkers in the tavern knew each other. Eavesdropping, Hendrick was drawn in.

"Dee is a villian, thrasonical and a sot." Arthur declared.

"He is Termagant." Nicholas nodded.

"He is yaw, yet he acts indifferent and is lewd." Thomas agreed.

"I heard he is a swinge-buckler, and a Setebos." Rupert whispered not so quietly.

"It is known that he is a skilless spial." They all agreed.

"Dee is spirited since Kelley left." Thomas whispered then.

"Don't be shrewd and scathful." Hendrick scolded. "Dr Dee is an audacious bawcock."

"You are a single ninny." Lionel said, pointing at Hendrick.

"He is a rook; a revolt; a rack of a man, nothing but a rag." Rupert spat.

"He is a prime patch." Arthur sneered.

"Like Ouphe, you are pardous but a motley-minded mome." Thomas said to Hendrick.

"Your mind is perdu with tales of the fanatical." Rupert agreed.

"You act greenly, you exsufficate dullard." Hendrick replied.

"You are nothing but a cowish geck in daub." Arthur declared.

"You are a capocchia." Hendrick replied.

"You are a caitiff of his, taken over by a bug; a bavin, just like the antick." He was told.

"He is a cozener, nothing but a quat." Lionel agreed.

"He tries to be the approver, but he is a zany." Thomas pointed out.

"Dr Dee is an inkhorn-mate, that is all." Hendrick shook his head.

"Mephistophilus delivers instructions to him directly." Lionel whispered.

"They say he is an anthropophaginian." Arthur added.

"He is a chamberer, a Popinjay." Lionel declared.

Rupert laughed. "So it is seated. He is a roisting, roynish, rubious rook!"

"You are nothing but a revolt; a ripe revolt." Hendrick shook his head.

Another man joined in. "He is diffused and dearn." Hendrick smiled at him, glad to have an ally.

"No, he is a facinorous espial." Arthur argued.

"You are a braid cracker." Hendrick was told.

Hendrick replied. "You are a lither loon."

"You are a meazel." Another man agreed, on Hendrick's side.

*13*

"You are a lag." Rupert replied.

Shaking his head, Hendrick got up from the table, walking across the room away from them all.

Rupert followed, stopping him. "You are forbode to use the jakes."

In response, Hendrick pushed him out of the way.

Rupert snarled. "That will cost you lief."

"A bung of lowre and you think you rule all!" One cried.

"Via!" Rupert shouted, consumed with yellowness. Hendrick didn't move.

"You are a beshrew!" Rupert screamed at him, holding the poniard level with Hendrick's face.

A flash of light caught the poinard as Rupert moved.

The whoo-bub fell whist whiles...

"What betid!" The ward watchman asked, hurrying into the tavern.

"There has been a grave occurent." Lionel told him.

"He's a serpent." Thomas claimed.

"What is this wroth?" The ward watchman boomed. Silence fell.

"Am I yare?" He asked.

They nodded, yarely, telling of the threats to stain him, which Hendrick ignored and how Hendrick was refusing to subscribe. The man with the poniard was very mistempered, and heady. They were gast, the eyewitnesses reported.

The watchman summoned the arch leech to tend to Hendrick's injuries, arresting Rupert and leaving the tavern with him.

The arch leech, sprag and point-de-vice, is an importing cavalero, commanding respect everywhere he went. Silence fell as he entered the tavern.

"He is bisson." The arch leech concluded to the crowd. "He must be allowed to recure." He advised, turning his attention to Hendrick.

"What is the tarriance? Act festinately. The pain is fineless." Hendrick groaned.

Have coragio, he was told.

He struggled to suspire his threne of thought. His expression uneath concealed his teen, his tire shading his face.

The skin had to be pieled before the neeld could be inserted. Hendrick passed out.

## 2.

The stranger tried to blend in, becoming a street higgler. From there, he watched – everything and everyone. There were plenty of artificers – a cozier, a costermonger, a currier and a cordwainer - in the vicinity. His expression was wailful. It was obvious he was voluble and of sufferance, his eyes holding a hidden wannion.

Dr Dee knew of him, and knew that he would be the one to tell him where to find Hendrick.

Having found Hendrick easily, Dee put his plan into action.

His actions would be successive because he was parted and parlous, and Dr Dee was orgulous of him.

Hendrick was rapt. He was filled with a palmy pudency: Dr Dee was orgulous of him.

With praise ringing in his ears, Hendrick's mouth fell open when Dr Dee offered him a position as his assistant. He agreed quickly.

By averring the agreement, there was nothing to baccare, Hendrick knew.

Dee was fain, his new assistant was forgetive and not exsufficate, as he was forspent. There would be no sense of emulation. He was in dich, yet distempered, distraught - and dry. He led his assistant to the tavern.

Confused, Hendrick followed, solemnly determined to have his master like him.

Looking around, Hendrick concluded there was a sense of capricious, a constant sense of complexion with a hint of cautel. Nobody inside was cautelous, just buxom with an audacious streak, tossing their statute-caps in the air in celebration.

He heard snatches of conversation:

"She is a no good gamester."

"He is nayward, he cannot be swayed."

"I do not wish to baffle you."

"He took in snuff straight."

Dee dropped his voice. "We must be alone to expostulate." However, he saw the questions in Hendrick's face, and encouraged him to speak.

"This is an agreement of commodity." Hendrick said airily. "I'm not franked and I am treated as more of a feere than a feeder."

Dee nodded. "Agreed."

# 3.

Hendrick tried to take in everything in Dee's lab, knowing that everything had an important purpose. In the corner stood a statua of unknown, and a state by a large sanded vase.

On the table amongst the horologe, unravalled inkle, the gad lay beside the pouncet-box and periapts lay on the table beside the perspective. The box was latten, unusual in it's design.

A pomander hung in the window, glistening in the light on a tundish, umbered but not vinewed, and a table-book. The table-book he saw was filled with strange symbols and mystical tales. Beside that, the three spheres clinquant in the light.

That was all he got to see as the room shouldered into darkness, yet there was a strange legerity around the room.

"There must be a steeled, still temperance in the room so that the material must be sheer and sere." Dee advised him. "My time must be continuate. Do not jut my space."

There was a pause and Hendrick wondered what was expected of him.

"After a long travail, the results are toward." Dee told him.

Katherine argued, but Hendrick didn't catch what she said.

"It is plausive. Nothing is point-de-vice." Dee told her.

Hendrick nodded.

18

"It is, at the moment, only a tested theorick." Dee pointed out.

Hendrick nodded again.

Katherine spoke then. "Father, why do you need this man?" Her voice was of sneap, spoke softly. Her expression was sorriest.

"He displayed a scantling of sheen." Dee replied.

"I shall not forspeak him. Your secrets will not be imbared." Hendrick promised her. His speech was sacrificial, Hendrick realised. Dee's words: "You are of skill" still were in his mind.

After that, he was left alone in the room with Katherine. His attention turned back to the table. Examining the smaller sphere: "There are strange denotements." Hendrick frowned.

Katherine explained. "It has been derived from the Gods."

"It is mere estimation!" Hendrick replied, his tone of bob.

Katherine shook her head.

"I do not fear being firked." Hendrick told her.

Amusement danced in her eyes. "You do not?"

He shook his head. "Tell me more." He gestured around the room.

"Everything is put away feater in order to find it in a hurry, even after a long gest." Katherine informed him, stopping him as he began. "Do not temper the two potions." Placing others in front of him, Katherine ordered. "Mell these together."

"It is quail," Hendrick frowned.

*19*

"It will fleet. Make sure it is seeled." She instructed. "Then limn and level the cuttle. Do not drumble, nor drive."

Frowning, she guided his shaky hands. Her touch so enthralled him, Hendrick failed to know Dee's presence.

Dee saw they had an immediacy, and did not like it.

"I know not who to trow." He snarled at Katherine in a rapture of rage. "It is up to you to project the young man. He cannot trow for himself."

Hendrick glut hastily, as Dr Dee continued his rant. The words caused him to knap and Hendrick escaped to the tavern's hurly.

Dee moved featly, gaberdine wrapped tightly around him to keep out the bitter wind, finding Hendrick in the corner of the tavern ten minutes later.

Looking up from his glass, Hendrick gave a regreet as Dee approached him.

"I will allow it if you are serious about Katherine."

Hendrick's jaw dropped open in shock.

"I must be the first to gratulate her. It must not be fub off." Dee shook his head, not waiting for the answer first. "Does that fadge you?"

Hendrick tried to englut. "Yes sir."

"Do not let her distaste you." He was warned.

He failed to glose, and was encouraged to finish his drink before returning.

Upon his return, across the room, Dee gave him a mop.

He wafted Hendrick over. "It needs to be tempered properly before allowed to quench." He instructed. "Don't forget to rake it."

"Yes sir." Hendrick replied, hoping this would be enough.

"It was rawly covered and it was frushed before." Dee explained.

Dee walked across the room to leave, pausing at Katherine's side. "You are pathetical." Dee told her.

His behaviour is moonish, Hendrick thought: knowing he was not allowed to glose.

Katherine distracted him when Dee left, telling him the story of how the place was rebuilt. The fire was set in the bay, and soon took hold. It destroyed half of the library at Mortlake before it was controlled.

"We feared all was perdu!" Katherine shook her head.

Hendrick nodded, feeling something was meant of him at her pause.

Katherine took a deep breath. "But there was no sense of denay, no condolement from father."

Hendrick frowned. "Did not that fester? You should be despatched by the loss."

Katherine shrugged. "It was primer that everyone escaped alive." In the silence, she looked at him. "Would you like to see it?"

Hendrick smiled at her, and followed her through the house, down the cranks to the library. He gasped when he saw the walls of books. Going closer, he could see that there were a lot that were written by Dr John Dee – counting, he found there were 49 in total.

"Queen Mary did not like the idea of having all books, manuscripts and records in one place when it was proposed in 1556." She spread her hands. "So it is here."

"Are there many visitors?" Hendrick asked.

Katherine nodded, watching him go to the shelves of Dr Dee's books. He paused at General and Rare Memorials pertayning to the Perfect Arte of Navigation.

"Father advised Queen Elizabeth on navigation and discovery in foreign lands by the British Empery for many years. He was the one who produced the term." She had a proud look in her eyes.

Putting the book back carefully, Hendrick then found a slimmer volume Monas Hieroglyphica. Opening it, he saw it contained lots of symbols. His frown told her that he didn't understand.

Katherine smiled at his confusion. "That one expresses the mystical unity of all creation."

Quickly, Hendrick replaced it on the shelf.

"There are many science works." Katherine pointed out De Trigono, Testamentum Johannis Dee Philosophi Summi ad Johannem Guryun Transmissum, An Account of the Manner in which a Certayn Copper-smith in the Land of Moores, and a Certayn Moore Transmuted Copper to Gold.

Hendrick saw also On The Mystical Rule of the Seven Planets, True and Faithful Relation of Dr

John Dee and Some Spirits by John Dee, Mysteriorum Liber Sextus et Sanctus, Compendium Heptarchiae Mysticae, De Heptarchia Mystica, Tuba Veneris... He shook his head, sure that these were above his understanding.

"I'm sure you would find father's diary of more interest." Katherine told him. "Ask him to show you." Hendrick smiled at her then.

## 4.

The weapon was hent as the instruction was given: Impeticos the poniard.
However, the watchman did not have the poniard when he arrived with Rupert in front of the beak.
"I am mated that you would impeach evidence." The beak told him.
Turning to the court, he began.
"It has been leged that nobody was incensed. Yet, several men told of threats from the accused to stain the victim despite his refusing to subscribe. Eyewitnesses were afeared and gast."
"I am sentenced to deem." Rupert moaned.
"The incident was intended to be a kindless lethe of a juvenal." The beak continued.
Rupert muttered for forgiveness.
"You are scathful and shrewd, and you seek shrift from me?" The beak shook his head.
"Where is your credit?" He said to the watchman.
He displayed a curstness, and read through the information. "Those candle-wasters, drunk on Charneco, talked loudly over the broken music, had an argument."
"He brought the poniard down with force over the man's face."
Rupert stuttered his apology.
"Your apology is lated." The beak peered at him over his spectacles. "I'm sending you to the derrick."

## 5.

The atmosphere was both of mood and inwardness, intentively indigest.
Hendrick knew that he looked indifferent, compared to Katherine - she was quaint. It was obvious she was not unbreathed.
Being fulsome made him emulous. He was flush and fancy-free. He gave oeilliad across to her...
It would be easier if she was sightless, he thought.
"I wouldn't want you to misthink of me." He said to her.
Her answer was mobled, but he heard it. "Find another way to fleet."
She attended to the vegetives; she was tight and yet stark, her expression tempered.
The conversation ended there. Silence fell for an hour until dinner.
"If I can make a prompture. We should capitulate."
He looked at her longly as she served their food.
"This is nothing but a drollery." She gave scall. "Here is your dole, and your pottage."
He was ravin, watching as she stooped to beteem the ale and sat beside him. Cutting a moiety of pie for afterwards. A tiny shive only.
"We shall convive." She declared.
He sighed inly. The lush meal was fit for a King.
His permanent defeature made him recognisable everywhere he went. But his refined yet bushy beard entranced her. Her beautiful long hair was

cain-coloured, her skin delicately pale. She knew men desired her. As he sneaped her bottom, it was obvious Hendrick was not oblivious to her charms.

He gave her a largess, a medal. Wooing her with words pleached with romanticism. Soon they were joined in couplement.

The jar was the first thing he was aware of.
"This should never be divulged." She warned.
"You have an extent of fact." He smiled.
She scowled.
"It was a quiddit, not a quip!" He explained.
"I find it an unnecessary taxing."
She crossed the room to the boitier vert, extracting from within the medal. There was no time to tender him and her feelings as there came a timeless knock. Wrapping the velure around her, she disappeared.

An hour later, she was forced to consort him to the wherry. "If that was to claw me,"
"I only meant to atone." He looked at her agazed.
Katherine nodded. "The password is: The Thames looks bollen today. You should reply: He arrived anight, he did not see."
Hendrick nodded, memorising the phrases as an argument broke out in the street below.
"It was but a bruit!"
"You are the bawd!"
The two men had hold of each other then.

"You have a chance to approve." She told him, drawing his attention back to her.

"I shall not forspeak him. I am in his depend." He reassured her. He stooped to inclip her. Even touching her tarred him. "Good-den," he tipped his hat to her, before leaving.

His tone caused her to quake. "It was my intention only to possess you." She whispered.

He took his seat on the wherry, smiling at her. "And I, you." Hendrick replied.

She quailed.

## 6.

London's best playwrights were all mewed up in the room. But there was no abhor until a brabble erupted amongst those in the room.

Augustus saw Humphrey admiring his reflection. "A sign of vainness in man means that he has a vailing validity."

"Sith your speech is skimble-skamble, he is tilly-vally!" Humphrey replied.

Laughter.

"Such a verbal man should be a scholar." William suggested.

"Are you unpregnant?" Humphrey turned to him.

"You would take up?" Leopold asked Humphrey.

"You are a troublesome squarer!" Humphrey replied.

"You are a fardel!" Augustus told him.

More laughter.

Ernest came into the room then. "What is this garboil?" He demanded.

Silence fell.

"I have a specially for you," he said to the playwrights. Ernest went on to explain, finishing the plan with: "It is a vastidity, a vast. It vaunt anything done before." He looked around the group.

"I intend to defy it." Leopold shouted.

"Were you previously under-wrought?" Augustus asked him.

"I intend to demerit." William murmured.

"Are you unquestionable?" Augustus asked William.

William shook his head, slipping out of the room as another brabble broke out.

"Do as you are seen, or your reputation will be forever smirched. No speed for you!" They were warned.

"It is too too tasking." Leopold shook his head.

The mood around the room was convinced.

"Convert your thinking." Ernest snapped at the playwrights. "You must cony-catch in order to colt the man." They were told.

"Remember the lines of the play need to be con." He ordered.

"We have been conned." Leopold shook his head sadly.

"Grave your fears." Ernest ordered. "Do not ban. In cope, you shall receive gimmal." He offered.

"Do not harry me or it will hack." Leopold tried.

"You dare me?" Ernest asked dangerously. "Via!"

"How about you?" Ernest looked at Humphrey and Augustus.

"No sir. I am in your depend." They responded meekly as Leopold left.

"To determine, I will design of relevance. You must not doff signing." Ernest instructed.

"I shall forbid the plan and I shall take the detect for setting everything in darraign." The statement read that each man had to sign.

"It is distaste." Humphrey whispered to Augustus.

"His behaviour was falsing." Augustus moaned, his expression was lumpish.

"The Master of the Revels has to agree." Humphrey reminded him.

"The plan is kam." Augustus shook his head.

"That is a fig!" Ernest shook his head.

"Don't be so judicious. The benefits countervail..." Humphrey began.

He was cut off. "My reputation will be collied."

"It is our co-mart." Ernest said, his eyes glinting dangerously.

"I am contrary," Augustus began. "How shall we convey?"

"Do not examine the plan." They were warned. "Your job is to propagate this onto others. Do not bodge it."

Silence fell.

Ernest reminded them as he got up to leave. "You signed the book, you are bound by its terms. It is bootless to argue."

# 7.

Augustus's and Humphrey's opinions hurtled as they created the abridgement between them. So each man wrote his own and agreed the scripts parcelled would be merged to form the play. Ernest did not let them leave the building until it was finished.

- 'The sky was nighted...'
- 'As night-rule...'

Pen down, Humphrey crossed his arms in front of his chest. "I shall not forspeak Dee." He shook his head.

"You agreed to holp. You did impeticos the money. Do not cause a foreslow." Augustus told him.

They both sighed.

"We shall impawn." Humphrey said after a moment. "I misdoubt there will be no indenting."

Augustus glut hastily, nodding: "He jades us."

"That does not matter as long as we are paid. And released." Humphrey pointed out. "He will be indited, not us." He continued.

"Nothing has been impeached. Nobody knows we are missing." Augustus pointed out.

- "Look at them. Jauncing and jetting on the stage!" Dee loffed.

"You should not loffe nor glose." He was told, before being dragged outside.

"You cannot renege me of my right!" Dee cried out.

"You should not repugn." He was told.

"I did not ask for your rate." Dee retorted.

The man tried another way. "Let's propose that you were asked to…"

Dee cut him off. "I wouldn't propose anything if I were you."

The man slapped Dee's cheek hard. "You need to limn the map of the Palace. Do not dare to refell."

Dee did as he was bade, writing down the ways in and out of the main gate beside the map.

"Is he telling the truth?" One asked.

"He swore a marry trap to tell the truth." Came the reply.

"He is too green to use his invention." Came another reply.

The man shook his head. "A tale of hardiment, but lies, all lies. Hence, Dee shall be known as horn-mad and under my hest. He shall be tried and punished - he shall be drowned in an ice-brook and sent to an eterne hell."

Scene at the Palace.

He tried to scan the papers but the writing was impossible to cipher.

"Scant the details!" The man was furious. "Why did you propose with him?"

"I was forced to consign." Dee said meekly. "I could not renege the deal."

"It is not simular?"

Dee shook his head. "The price on her head is rated at more than gimmal."

"So, it was included…?" The question hung in the air.

"The Queen must fall." Dee's words were uttered through clenched teeth. He shook his head. "Language must be qualified. The palabras will be paid." He stared sans remorse, although his ostentation was normal.

"It was a ratolorum; a practise that nobody dared question." He eyed Dee. "You give no hint, no thought!"

"I am but the missive. If the fault is mine, I will be shent." Dee told him.

He, mammering, thought for a while before eating the marchpanes in silence. A mess of men, who didn't like to deal with the metaphysical. Their actions were meacock, but full of mallecho. The man angled his head. "Forgive my misprision. You must display the utmost hugger-mugger about this."

"We have to unclew this." Dee ordered.

"Your thoughts are immoment." He snapped.

Dee smiled. "The detail is incony and intrinse. But it is a gimmor. I will wreak this."

- There was an interruption to the play then, a loud noise.

The loud noise was a rift in the scaffoldage.

"You have gain-givings?" The main player said to the groundlings, who ran out as one.

"Yes!" They screamed.

Within minutes, the fire confounded the theatre. The men of the fire service were warned to the burning theatre. They completed a rigol around the fire, prest and waiting. Alas, it was a planched structure and all of the polled wood was seared.

*33*

"It is composed. The theatre shall be cogged." The head firemarshall said to the mayor.
"Show some expedience!" He barked at his men.

- Rumour of Dee setting a curse upon the theatre.
"No provision had been made by Dee." He was told.
"Nonetheless, the plan, it is expiate." Came the reply.
In the silence, his shout of esperance echoed in the enemies ears.
"It is typical of Dee's chare." One man shook his head.
"His reputation will be latched." One man pointed out.
One whispered. "He was famous for his ability to prenominate."
"Was." One man snorted. "Not anymore."
He had to sowl Dee's unconscious body through the building, making sure the chains were sperred tightly before he was potched over the outer wall and left to hang.
"Quicken now." He snarled, laughing.
He nicked the plan. "He cannot be killed. He will reduce secrets from the dead."
"He created a nick and will accite the Devil."
The men gleeked.
"Do not gleek." They were lectured.
"This is set up to gallow us." He shook his head.
"I had prevented something like this. I shall quote this."

Another man shook his head. "I will take no part in such patchery."

"I will let God deliver the rate." One man agreed.

"He is forever making a calculate or a ceremony." One man shuddered. "The strange events are of moe."

"I hear Dee spends his time in laystalls and stews." One man confessed in a whisper.

"It is eld. Soon he will be derogate to beg and take up."

"He shall be damned. Send him to Bedlam!" Rose the chant.

A missive arrived. "He is amort. It has been erewhile they did grave him."

Silence fell.

- End of play

Ernest was, overall, pleased with the work, and released Augustus and Humphrey, who ran into the daylight as if they hadn't seen it before.

# 8.

"Pall the barrel, and it will expulse the air harmlessly. Try to eche, it takes time to reload." Dee told him.

Hendrick nodded, and concentrated, aiming the firearm at the target as Dee had before him.

Katherine was present to keep nick.

The nether-stocks and a kirtle made of lockram itched. Beneath the kirtle, slops are worn, but it still itched. Hendrick tried to ignore the uncomfortable itch from his new clothes.

"Pull back the hammer. It must be factious, expedient." Dee instructed.

Hendrick's hands shook so much he couldn't fire it. He lowered the firearm and shook his head.

"What happened?" Katherine asked.

"I failed to rive the weapon. It is my misprise." Hendrick bowed his head.

In truth, he was too overwhelmed – taken into the family home, given food and money and clothing, trusted with all of Dr Dee's secrets, in relationship with his daughter. Things were going too fast.

"No matter." Katherine smiled at him. "Father will take you to the tavern for a drink."

Dee looked at her in shock, but nodded when Hendrick looked up at him.

At the tavern, they sat in the corner and Hendrick listened to the conversation around them.

"Gallow them off the scent." Came the instruction.

"Sperr for the border."

"It will not work, you will be reduced."

"His expression was mortal."

"It was a rash quell." One man pointed out.

"He was of a lower ordinance, a miscreate." He shrugged.

"That doesn't make it right." He replied.

"What gives you the right to censure?"

He refused to parle on the subject any more, noting Hendrick was listening.

Hendrick's attention returned to Dee, noticing that everyone was looking at them then.

"It is unhatched, not to be unproper. We see why now. Look to welkin. It is written in the blackness of the stars." The man muttered, and moved away from them.

"He is an irregulous jack." Hendrick shook his head.

"He's nothing but a lowt; an immoment lewdster you must pay no attention to." Dee told him. "It is no secret that they all misprise me."

Sending several looks to those peering at them soon brought peace.

Dee attracted the attention of the musicians in the corner.

"Give us a cital? Certes!" The leader instructed his players to begin playing jovial.

Nothing could be heard over the broken music, which was how Dee liked it.

## 9.

"It is degrees in the right direction." Hendrick agreed.

"Stop digressing." Dee told him. "With a dowle your attention is gone!" He shook his head. "The empery is under threat!" Dee warned. "The information was most importing."

Shaking his head, he looked at Hendrick. "It is your job to find out the plan."

Hendrick nodded.

"I shall protect her Majesty." Dee told him, and disappeared.

"Such strange currents, whatever is going on at the Palace?" The crowd asked.

The coat of arms above the door was bold and of gules. The hubbub reached the receiving hall where Dee was explaining. "The danger is crescive, her Majesty must be informed." Dee insisted. "She will be safe with an armed convoy at cock-shut-time."

The order came: "Coast the plan!"

"Such a plan is not eft," her Majesty began, following the man as he took the cranks in the Palace cellars to the secret hideaway.

The chant rose. "The Palace shall be convinced."

He tripped on the path's coign, stumbled and caught himself. Hugging the wall cantle so as not to be seen as he approached the bourn, Hendrick hid behind a crumbled mure, listening.

*38*

"Everything was in darraign, but I shall not be daffed." Hendrick said to himself. "I shall not drive." He thought to himself: "This is a terrible hap to take." He shook his head. "I hope I will never be hight on it."

Then, he heard their leader speak. "When I give the imposition, you will leap into action without indurance."

Hendrick's eyes widened. He hadn't believed the plan until then.

"Who is here making inquistions?" Dee frowned.

"It is I, intending the Queen."

There was an intermission between the two men.

"It is a trick. It is him who wishes her Majesty harm!" One man declared, pointing at Dee.

Shaking his head, Dee sighed. "I would never and I do not weet the plan to take in the Palace."

"We will make him shrive." A Palace guard said.

Dee muttered under his breath.

"He's using some kind of code. He's using castiliano vulgo." They exclaimed.

"Qualify your tone." Dee told him.

Silence fell.

## 10.

"What betid?" The bellman asked.

The tavern owner spoke. "They say he is nothing but an unbolted trojan, paying with a supposed stay!"

"He is a lifter." The other man shook his head, waving his cuttle at the accused.

"Sheath your cuttle or I shall have you set up for a shoulder-clapping." The bellman said.

The headborough took charge from the bellman, threatening the thief with engines and pilliwinks before the beak would send him to the derrick.

"The charge is converyance. I will only need to attend quartan." The thief sneered.

He received a slap around the head to quieten him.

"Is there a meed?" The bellman was asked: he laughed.

## 11.

The group was operant here, that was obvious. Hendrick hid when he saw three men approach.
"Contrary to belief, this is a mere cognizance." One man said.
The instruction came then: "You must mammock the stone."
"That is offering." One man sighed.
"Frush it? We must fordo it." The first voice replied.
It was be-moiled to hide it. Hendrick watched from his hiding place.
"We must conster the truth. And not cozen." The first man said.
"It will countervail." Another shook his head.
"It is a matter of home urgency." The first man urged. "There is no corollary. Do it!"
Once the group had gone, Hendrick dug up the stone, seeing several symbols on it that he recognised. He knew then he had to take it to show Dr Dee and Katherine.

## 12.

The farced head of a stag in one corner watched everyone in the room. They all wore chopin and a copatain hat, and a rabato. In Winter, their hats and gloves of cheveril kept them warm.

"It is your job to impress the guests." The blue-coat was told.

A blue-coat stacked firing by the fireplace before shaking the napery over the table before the guests arrived for dinner.

Serving the meal, he couldn't help but overhear the conversations.

"There have been several grave occurents." The master of the house paused for effect. "The gardens are paled, for security."

The men shook their heads in disgust. "Amongst them, we must have mealed." One man shuddered.

Their meal passed pleasantly.

"Have a biggen before you leave." They were bade.

Not one of them failed to enjoy the biggen, he saw.

## 13.

In Dee's lab, Hendrick laid the stone on the table for him and Katherine to examine: they took it to another room.

It was then he saw the papers on time travel and wormholes, although he did not understand them. They were half under the working that Dr Dee called a calendar. It was another great work that Hendrick did not understand.

When Dr Dee returns, he is reading the papers.

"You are a braid, motley-minded mome." Dee told him, mistempered.

Hendrick's expression was wailful and he was afeared. "I am sorriest for my gain-givings."

Mammering, Dee accepts his apology.

"I want to learn more." Hendrick whispered.

Dee showed him extracts in his diary then, telling tales of hardiment from lands far away.

"My stay with the geographer, Gerardus Mercator, was more than a fleet. He produced an atlas, a book with maps from all over the world. Such a complement."

Hendrick nodded.

"He gave me a largess of the latten staff and globes." Dee pointed to the items.

"The communication crystal from Uriel the angel is a gaze." Hendrick said then.

Dee nodded wisely.

"After the occurents of a new star and a comet, my know helped Queen Elizabeth to build a great Navy

*43*

under Drake. They had quiddits and promptures, but were prone to capitulate."

"What other complements have you made?" Hendrick asked after a while.

Dee smiled. "I agreed to holp James Burbage in the building of the Theatre. After his lethe, his sons had to cog the building anight and rebuilt it as the Globe in Southwark."

Hendrick's mouth dropped open in shock.

"In the future, there will be no need for a wherry, there will be a tunnel under the Thames." Dee told him, smiling at his shock. "I can prenominate the future."

"What else will happen in the future?" Hendrick asked.

"Many importing finds." Dee said.

"And?"

"The palabras of the metaphysical will be festinately forbode." Dee shook his head.

A thought struck Hendrick. "Will you be able to travel to the future?"

Dee nodded wisely.

Hendrick stared at him agazed.

## Part 2 written in modern English terminology

# 1.

Outside, the ward (one of the 26 areas into which the City of London is divided for local administration) watchman (parish officer appointed to patrol the streets by night) strode by, walking his route up to the City gate and back again.

The pickpocket, the cutpurse and their accomplices who identify and distract victims skirted the pools of dark, biding their time.

Hendrick looked around, seeing faces that he didn't recognise and some that he did, realising that most of the drinkers in the tavern knew each other. Eavesdropping, Hendrick was drawn in.

"Dee is a low born man, boastful and a fool." Arthur declared.

"He is Termagant (a ranting character in old plays)." Nicholas nodded.

"He is out of control, yet he acts ordinary and ignorant." Thomas agreed.

"I heard he is a bully, and a Setebos (the name of a fiend)." Rupert whispered not so quietly.

"It is known that he is an ignorant spy." They all agreed.

"Dee is haunted since Kelley left." Thomas whispered then.

"Don't be mischievious and destructive." Hendrick scolded. "Dr Dee is a daring, fine fellow."

"You are a feeble fool." Lionel said, pointing at Hendrick.

47

"He is a cheater, a rebel; a wreck of a man, nothing but a rag (term of contempt)." Rupert spat.

"He is a lecherous, mean fellow." Arthur sneered.

"Like Ouphe (a fairy), you are perilously keen but a foolish stupid person." Thomas said to Hendrick.

"Your mind is lost with tales of the fanatical." Rupert agreed.

"You act foolishly, you contemptible dull person." Hendrick replied.

"You are nothing but a cowardly fool in disguise." Arthur declared.

"You are a simpleton." Hendrick replied.

"You are a captive of his, taken over by a spectre; worthless, just like the fool in old plays." He was told.

"He is a confidence trickster, nothing but a pimple." Lionel agreed.

"He tries to be the one who proves, but he is a clown." Thomas pointed out.

"Dr Dee is a man of learning and hated for it, that is all." Hendrick shook his head.

"Mephistophilus (the name of a familiar spirit) delivers instructions to him directly." Lionel whispered.

"He is an effeminate man, a conceited overly fashionable man." Lionel declared.

Rupert laughed. "So it is confirmed. He is a violent, mangy, ruddy cheater!"

"You are nothing but a rebel; a drunk rebel." Hendrick shook his head.

Another man joined in. "He is confused and lonely."

Hendrick smiled at him, glad to have an ally.

"No, he is a wicked spy." Arthur argued.

"You are a deceitful boaster." Hendrick was told.

Hendrick replied. "You are a lazy low contemptible fellow."

"You are a mean person." Another man agreed, on Hendrick's side.

"You are the lowest of people." Rupert replied.

Shaking his head, Hendrick got up from the table, walking across the room away from them all.

Rupert followed, stopping him. "You are forbidden to use the privy."

In response, Hendrick pushed him out of the way.

Rupert snarled. "That will cost you dear."

"A pocket of coin and you think you rule all!" One cried.

"Off with you!" Rupert shouted, consumed with jealousy.

Hendrick didn't move.

"You are an evil befal!" Rupert screamed at him, holding the dagger level with Hendrick's face.

A flash of light caught the dagger as Rupert moved. The hubbub fell silent until...

"What happened!" The officer asked, hurrying into the tavern.

"There has been a grave incident." Lionel told him.

"He's a worm." Thomas claimed.

"What is this calamity?" The officer boomed.

Silence fell.

"Am I being understood?" He asked.

They nodded, readily, telling of the threats to disfigure him, which Hendrick ignored and how Hendrick was refusing to succumb. The man with the dagger was very angry, and violent. They were frightened, the eyewitnesses reported.

The watchman summoned the chief physician to tend to Hendrick's injuries, arresting Rupert and leaving the tavern with him.

The chief physician, quick and faultless, is a significant gentleman, commanding respect everywhere he went. Silence fell as he entered the tavern.

"He is blind." The chief physician concluded to the crowd. "He must be allowed to recover." He advised, turning his attention to Hendrick.

"What is the delay? Act quickly. The pain is endless." Hendrick groaned.

Have courage, he was told.

He struggled to breathe his lament of grief. His expression hardly concealed his grief, his head dress (attire) shading his face.

The skin had to be shaven before the needle could be inserted. Hendrick passed out.

## 2.

The foreigner tried to blend in, becoming a street peddlar. From there, he watched – everything and everyone. There were plenty of skilled workmen – a tailor, a stall holder (especially selling fruit), a craftsman who turns skins into leather and a worker in the best leather - in the vicinity. His expression was lamentable. It was obvious he was fickle and suffering, his eyes holding a hidden vengence.

Dr Dee knew of him, and knew that he would be the one to tell him where to find Hendrick.

Having found Hendrick easily, Dee put his plan into action.

His actions would be succeeding because he was gifted and shrewd, and Dr Dee was proud of him.

Hendrick was transported with emotion. He was filled with a victorious modesty: Dr Dee was proud of him.

With praise ringing in his ears, Hendrick's mouth fell open when Dr Dee offered him a position as his assistant. He agreed quickly.

By confirming the agreement, there was nothing to keep back, Hendrick knew.

Dee was glad his new assistant was inventive and not contemptible, as he was exhausted. There would be no sense of jealousy. He was in an optative mood, yet discontented, distracted - and thirsty. He led his assistant to the tavern.

Confused, Hendrick followed, solemnly determined to have his master like him.

Looking around, Hendrick concluded there was a sense of lascivious, a determined sense of passion with a hint of deceit. Nobody inside was insidious, just obedient with a spirited streak, tossing their woollen caps in the air in celebration.

He heard snatches of conversation:

"She is a no good frolicsome person, a loose woman."

"He is towards denial, he cannot be swayed."

"I do not wish to embarrass you."

"He took offence immediately."

Dee dropped his voice. "We must be alone to discuss." (to expostulate is to set forth or state in detail - ie to expound theories. or to explain.) However, he saw the questions in Hendrick's face, and encouraged him to speak.

"This is an agreement of convenience." Hendrick said airily. "I'm not confined and I am treated as more of a companion than a servant."

Dee nodded. "Agreed."

# 3.

Hendrick tried to take in everything in Dee's lab, knowing that everything had an important purpose. In the corner stood a statue of unknown, and a canopied chair by a large vase marked with yellow spots.

On the table amongst the clock, unravalled narrow tape, the pointed instrument lay beside the box for holding perfumes and charms worn round the neck lay on the table beside the telescope. The box was made of brass, unusual in it's design.

A perfumed ball hung in the window, glistening in the light on a funnel, stained but not mouldy, and a notebook. The notebook he saw was filled with strange symbols and mystical reckonings. Beside that, the three spheres glittered in the light.

That was all he got to see as the room plunged into darkness, yet there was a strange lightness around the room.

"There must be a set, constant temperature in the room so that the material must be dry and unmixed." Dee advised him. "My time must be uninterrupted. Do not encroach my space."

There was a pause and Hendrick wondered what was expected of him.

"After a long toil, the results are nearly ready." Dee told him.

Katherine argued, but Hendrick didn't catch what she said.

"It is plausible. Nothing is faultless." Dee told her.

Hendrick nodded.

"It is, at the moment, only a pure theory." Dee pointed out.

Hendrick nodded again.

Katherine spoke then. "Father, why do you need this man?" Her voice was of sarcasm, spoke gently. Her expression was most sorrowful.

"He displayed a small portion of brilliancy." Dee replied.

"I shall not speak against him. Your secrets will not be bared." Hendrick promised her.

His speech was reverent, as words used in religious worship, Hendrick realised. Dee's words: "You are of importance" still were in his mind.

After that, he was left alone in the room with Katherine. His attention turned back to the table. Examining the smaller sphere: "There are strange markings." Hendrick frowned.

Katherine explained. "It has descended from the Gods."

"It is mere conjecture!" Hendrick replied, his tone of sarcasm.

Katherine shook her head.

"I do not fear being severely chastised." Hendrick told her.

Amusement danced in her eyes. "You do not?"

He shook his head. "Tell me more." He gestured around the room.

"Everything is put away neatly in order to find it in a hurry, even after a long period." Katherine informed him, stopping him as he began. "Do not mix the two potions." Placing others in front of him, Katherine ordered. "Mix these together."

"It is languid," Hendrick frowned.

"It will float. Make sure it is closed." She instructed. "Then draw and aim the knife. Do not dwaddle, nor rush impetuously."

Frowning, she guided his shaky hands. Her touch so enthralled him, Hendrick failed to acknowledge Dee's presence.

Dee saw they had a close connection, and did not like it.

"I know not who to trust." He snarled at Katherine in a fit of rage. "It is up to you to shape the young man. He cannot think for himself."

Hendrick swallowed hastily, as Dr Dee continued his rant. The words caused him to crack and Hendrick escaped to the tavern's noise and confusion.

Dee moved nimbly, outer coat wrapped tightly around him to keep out the bitter wind, finding Hendrick in the corner of the tavern ten minutes later.

Looking up from his glass, Hendrick gave a salutation as Dee approached him.

"I will allow it if you are serious about Katherine." Hendrick's jaw dropped open in shock.

"I must be the first to congratulate her. It must not be put off." Dee shook his head, not waiting for the answer first. "Does that suit you?"

Hendrick tried to swallow speedily. "Yes sir."

"Do not let her corrupt you." He was warned.

He failed to comment, and was encouraged to finish his drink before returning.

Upon his return, across the room, Dee gave him a nod.

He beckoned Hendrick over. "It needs to be mixed properly before allowed to grow cool." He instructed. "Don't forget to cover it."

"Yes sir." Hendrick replied, hoping this would be enough.

"It was inadequately covered and was bruised before." Dee explained.

Dee walked across the room to leave, pausing at Katherine's side. "You are hypocritical." Dee told her.

His behaviour is inconstant, Hendrick thought: knowing he was not allowed to comment.

Katherine distracted him when Dee left, telling him the story of how the place was rebuilt. The fire was set in the space between the main timbers of the roof, and soon took hold. It destroyed half of the library at Mortlake before it was controlled.

"We feared all was lost!" Katherine shook her head.

Hendrick nodded, feeling something was meant of him at her pause.

Katherine took a deep breath. "But there was no sense of denial, no grief from father."

Hendrick frowned. "Did not that rankle? You should be bereaved by the loss."

Katherine shrugged. "It was more important that everyone escaped alive."

In the silence, she looked at him. "Would you like to see it?"

Hendrick smiled at her, and followed her through the house, down the winding passages to the library. He gasped when he saw the walls of books. Going closer, he could see that there were a lot that were written by Dr John Dee – counting, he found there were 49 in total.

"Queen Mary did not like the idea of having all books, manuscripts and records in one place when it was proposed in 1556." She spread her hands. "So it is here."

"Are there many visitors?" Hendrick asked.

Katherine nodded, watching him go to the shelves of Dr Dee's books. He paused at General and Rare Memorials pertayning to the Perfect Arte of Navigation.

"Father advised Queen Elizabeth on navigation and discovery in foreign lands by the British Empire for many years. He was the one who produced the term." She had a proud look in her eyes.

Putting the book back carefully, Hendrick then found a slimmer volume Monas Hieroglyphica. Opening it, he saw it contained lots of symbols. His frown told her that he didn't understand.

Katherine smiled at his confusion. "That one expresses the mystical unity of all creation."

Quickly, Hendrick replaced it on the shelf.

"There are many science works." Katherine pointed out De Trigono, Testamentum Johannis Dee Philosophi Summi ad Johannem Guryun Transmissum, An Account of the Manner in which a Certayn Copper-smith in the Land of Moores, and a Certayn Moore Transmuted Copper to Gold.

Hendrick saw also On The Mystical Rule of the Seven Planets, True and Faithful Relation of Dr John Dee and Some Spirits by John Dee, Mysteriorum Liber Sextus et Sanctus, Compendium Heptarchiae Mysticae, De Heptarchia Mystica, Tuba Veneris... He shook his head, sure that these were above his understanding.

"I'm sure you would find father's diary of more interest." Katherine told him. "Ask him to show you." Hendrick smiled at her then.

# 4.

The weapon was seized as the instruction was given: Pocket the dagger.

However, the officer did not have the dagger when he arrived with Rupert in front of the magistate.

"I am dismayed that you would bring into question evidence." The judge told him.

Turning to the court, he began.

"It has been alleged that nobody was incited. Yet, several men told of threats from the accused to disfigure the victim despite his refusing to succumb. Eyewitnesses were afraid and frightened."

"I am sentenced to doom." Rupert moaned.

"The incident was intended to be an unnatural death of a young man." The magistrate continued.

Rupert muttered for forgiveness.

"You are destructive and mischievous, and you seek absolution from me?" The magistrate shook his head.

"Where is your report?" He said to the officer.

He displayed a shrewishness, and read through the information. "Those persons who sit up all night to drink, drunk on Charneco (a sweet wine), talked loudly over the music of stringed instruments, had an argument."

"He brought the dagger down with force over the man's face."

Rupert stuttered his apology.

"Your apology is belated." The magistrate peered at him over his spectacles. "I'm sending you to the hangman."

# 5.

The atmosphere was both of anger and intimacy, attentively disordered.

Hendrick knew that he looked ordinary, compared to Katherine - she was curiously beautiful. It was obvious she was not unpracticed.

Being lustful made him jealous. He was full of vigour and untouched by love. He gave an amorous glance across to her...

It would be easier if she was unsightly, he thought.

"I wouldn't want you to think ill of me." He said to her.

Her answer was muffled, but he heard it. "Find another way to pass the time."

She attended to the herbs; she was stiff and yet nimble, her expression mixed.

The conversation ended there. Silence fell for an hour until dinner.

"If I can make a suggestion. We should work together." He looked at her longingly as she served their food.

"This is nothing but a puppet show." She gave a word of reproach. "Here is your free allowance of bread, and your stew."

He was ravenous, watching as she stooped to pour out the ale and sat beside him. Cutting a portion of pie for afterwards. A tiny slice only.

"We shall feast together." She declared.

He sighed inwardly. The luxuriant meal was fit for a King.

His permanent disfigurement made him recognisable everywhere he went. But his bolted yet bushy beard entranced her. Her beautiful long hair was red coloured, her skin delicately pale. She knew men desired her. As he pinched her bottom, it was obvious Hendrick was not oblivious to her charms.

He gave her a present, a portrait in a locket. Wooing her with words interwoven with romanticism. Soon they were joined in union.

The ticking of the clock was the first thing he was aware of.

"This should never be spoken of." She warned.

"You have a seizure of guilt." He smiled.

She scowled.

"It was a subtle question, not a taunt!" He explained.

"I find it an unnecessary satire."

She crossed the room to the green box, extracting from within the portrait in a locket. There was no time to have consideration for him and her feelings, as there came an untimely knock. Wrapping the velvet around her, she disappeared.

An hour later, she was forced to accompany him to the small river crossing boat. "If that was to flatter me,"

"I only meant to put people at one." He looked at her in amazement.

Katherine nodded. "The password is: The Thames looks swollen today. You should reply: He arrived by night, he did not see."

Hendrick nodded, memorising the phrases as an argument broke out in the street below.

"It was but a rumour!"

"You are the procurer!"

The two men had hold of each other then.

"You have a chance to make good." She told him, drawing his attention back to her.

"I shall not speak against him. I am in his service." He reassured her. He stooped to embrace her. Even touching her excited him. "Good evening," he tipped his hat to her, before leaving.

His tone caused her to tremble.

"It was my intention only to inform you." She whispered.

He took his seat on the small boat, smiling at her. "And I, you." Hendrick replied.

She fainted.

## 6.

London's best playwrights were all confined in the room. But there was no protest until a quarrel erupted amongst those in the room.

Augustus saw Humphrey admiring his reflection. "A sign of vanity in man means that he has a lowering value."

"Since your speech is rambling, he is tilly-vally!" (an exclamation of contempt.) Humphrey replied.

Laughter.

"Such a wordy man should be a scholar." William suggested.

"Are you stupid?" Humphrey turned to him.

"You would make up a quarrel?" Leopold asked Humphrey.

"You are a troublesome quarreller!" Humphrey replied.

"You are a burden!" Augustus told him.

More laughter.

Ernest came into the room then. "What is this disorder?" He demanded.

Silence fell.

"I have a special contract for you," he said to the playwrights. Ernest went on to explain, finishing the plan with: "It is an immensity, a gulf. It precedes anything done before." He looked around the group.

"I intend to renounce it!" Leopold shouted.

"Were you previously undermined?" Augustus asked him.

"I intend to desert." William murmured.

"Are you not inquisitive?" Augustus asked William.

William shook his head, slipping out of the room as another quarrel broke out.

"Do as you are instructed, or your reputation will be forever soiled. No fortune for you!" They were warned.

"It is excessively challenging." Leopold shook his head.

The mood around the room was subdued.

"Change your thinking." Ernest snapped at the playwrights.

"You must cheat in order to befool the man." They were told.

"Remember the lines of the play need to be learnt by heart." He ordered.

"We have been deceived." Leopold shook his head sadly.

"Bury your fears." Ernest ordered. "Do not curse. In return, you shall receive double." He offered.

"Do not harass me or it will become common." Leopold tried.

"You challenge me?" Ernest asked dangerously. "Off with you!"

"How about you?" Ernest looked at Humphrey and Augustus.

"No sir. I am in your service." They responded meekly as Leopold left.

"To conclude, I will draw up articles of relevance. You must not put off signing." Ernest instructed.

"I shall defend the plan and I shall take the blame for setting everything in array." The statement read that each man had to sign.

"It is corrupt." Humphrey whispered to Augustus.

"His behaviour was deceptive." Augustus moaned, his expression was dejected.

"The Master of the Revels has to agree. (organizer of royal entertainments and official censor.)" Humphrey reminded him.

"The plan is crooked." Augustus shook his head.

"That is an insult!" Ernest shook his head.

"Don't be so critical. The benefits outweigh..." Humphrey began.

He was cut off. "My reputation will be blackened."

"It is our joint bargain." Ernest said, his eyes glinting dangerously.

"I am opposed," Augustus began. "How shall we manage?"

"Do not question the plan." They were warned. "Your job is to forward this onto others. Do not botch it."

Silence fell.

Ernest reminded them as he got up to leave. "You signed the papers of conditions, you are bound by its terms. It is useless to argue."

# 7.

Augustus's and Humphrey's opinions clashed as they created the short play between them. So each man wrote his own and agreed that the scripts belonging to individuals would be merged to form the play.

Ernest did not let them leave the building until it was finished.

- 'The sky was black as night...'
- 'As nightly solemnity...'

Pen down, Humphrey crossed his arms in front of his chest. "I shall not speak against Dee." He shook his head.

"You agreed to help. You did pocket the money. Do not cause a delay." Augustus told him.

They both sighed.

"We shall compromise." Humphrey said after a moment. "I suspect there will be no bargaining."

Augustus swallowed hastily, nodding: "He treats us with contempt."

"That does not matter as long as we are paid. And released." Humphrey pointed out. "He will be convicted, not us." He continued.

"Nothing has been brought into question. Nobody knows we are missing." Augustus pointed out.

- "Look at them. Prancing and strutting on the stage!" Dee laughed.

"You should not laugh nor comment." He was told, before being dragged outside.

"You cannot deny me of my right." Dee cried out.

"You should not resist." He was told.

"I did not ask for your opinion." Dee retorted.

The man tried another way. "Let's say for the sake of argument that you were asked to…"

Dee cut him off. "I wouldn't suppose anything if I were you."

The man slapped Dee's cheek hard. "You need to draw the map of the Palace. Do not dare to refute."

Dee did as he was bade, writing down the ways in and out of the main gate beside the map.

"Is he telling the truth?" One asked.

"He swore an oath to tell the truth." Came the reply.

"He is too immature to use his imagination." Came another reply.

The man shook his head. "A tale of defiance and brave deeds, but lies, all lies. Henceforth, Dee shall be known as brain-mad and under my command. He shall be tried and punished - he shall be drowned in an icy cold brook and sent to an eternal hell."

Scene at the Palace.

He tried to examine subtly the papers, but the writing was impossible to decipher.

"Spare the details!" The man was furious. "Why did you converse with him?"

"I was forced to sign a common bond." Dee said meekly. "I could not renounce the deal."

"It is not feigned?"

Dee shook his head. "The price on her head is valued at more than double."

"So, it was concluded...?" The question hung in the air.

"The Queen must fall." Dee's words were uttered through clenched teeth. He shook his head. "Language must be moderated. The words will be punished." He stared without pity, although his appearance was normal.

"It was a ludicrous mistake; a wicked stratagem that nobody dared question." He eyed Dee. "You give no suggestion, no thought!"

"I am but the messenger. If the fault is mine, I will be rebuked." Dee told him.

He, hesitating, thought for a while before eating the sweet biscuits in silence. A company of four men, who didn't like to deal with the supernatural. Their actions were cowardly, but full of mischief. The man angled his head. "Forgive my mistake. You must display the utmost secrecy about this."

"We have to undo this." Dee ordered.

"Your thoughts are unimportant." He snapped.

Dee smiled. "The detail was fine, delicate and intricate. But it is a contrivance. I will avenge this."

- There was an interruption to the play then, a loud noise.

The loud noise was a split in the gallery of a theatre.

"You have misgivings?" The main player said to the groundlings (those who sit in the pit of a theatre), who ran out as one.

"Yes!" They screamed.

Within minutes, the fire consumed the theatre. The men of the fire service were summoned to the burning theatre. They completed a circle around the fire, ready and waiting. Alas, it was a structure made of boards and all of the bare wood was scorched or withered.

"It is agreed. The theatre shall be dissembled." The head firemarshall said to the mayor.

"Show some expedition (haste)!" He barked at his men.

- Rumour of Dee setting a curse upon the theatre.

"No forecast had been made by Dee." He was told.

"Nonetheless, the plan, it is complete." Came the reply.

In the silence, his war cry echoed in the enemies ears.

"It is typical of Dee's turn of work." One man shook his head.

"His reputation will be smeared." One man pointed out.

One whispered. "He was famous for his ability to prophesy."

"Was." One man snorted. "Not anymore."

He had to drag Dee's unconscious body through the building, making sure the chains were fastened tightly before he was pushed violently over the wall and left to hang.

"Come to life now." He snarled, laughing.

He branded with folly the plan. "He cannot be killed. He will bring back secrets from the dead."

"He tried to create a reckoning and will summon the Devil."

The men scoffed.

"Do not scoff." They were lectured.

"This is set up to scare us." He shook his head.

"I had anticipated something like this. I shall note this."

Another man shook his head. "I will take no part in such trickery."

"I will let God deliver the judgement." One man agreed.

"He is forever making a calculate or a ceremony." One man shuddered. "The strange events are of frequent occurrence."

"I hear Dee spends his time in dung heaps and brothels." One man confessed in a whisper.

"It is old age. Soon he will be degraded to beg and borrow money."

"He shall be condemned. Send him to Bedlam! (Bedlam - Bethlehem Hospital for the deranged.)" Rose the chant.

A messenger arrived. "He is dead. It has been a short time since they did bury him."

Silence fell.

- End of play

Ernest was, overall, pleased with the work, and released Augustus and Humphrey, who ran into the daylight as if they hadn't seen it before.

## 8.

"Wrap the barrel and it will expel the air harmlessly. Try to eke out, it takes time to reload." Dee told him. Hendrick nodded, and concentrated, aiming the firearm at the target as Dee had before him.

Katherine was present to keep score.

The stockings and a gown made of loose linen itched. Beneath the gown, loose breeches are worn, but it still itched. Hendrick tried to ignore the uncomfortable itch from his new clothes.

"Pull back the hammer. It must be instant, swift." Dee instructed.

Hendrick's hands shook so much he couldn't fire it. He lowered the firearm and shook his head.

"What happened?" Katherine asked.

"I failed to fire the weapon. It is my mistake." Hendrick bowed his head.

In truth, he was too overwhelmed – taken into the family home, given food and money and clothing, trusted with all of Dr Dee's secrets, in relationship with his daughter. Things were going too fast.

"No matter." Katherine smiled at him. "Father will take you to the tavern for a drink."

Dee looked at her in shock, but nodded when Hendrick looked up at him.

At the tavern, they sat in the corner and Hendrick listened to the conversation around them.

"Scare them off the scent." Came the instruction. "Bolt for the border."

"It will not work, you will be brought back."

"His expression was murderous."

"It was a violent murder." One man pointed out.

"He was of a lower rank, an illegitimate." He shrugged.

"That doesn't make it right." He replied.

"What gives you the right to criticise?"

He refused to talk on the subject any more, noting Hendrick was listening.

Hendrick's attention returned to Dee, noticing that everyone was looking at them then.

"It is undisclosed, not to be common to all. We see why now. Look to the sky. It is written in the blackness of the stars." The man muttered, and moved away from them.

"He is a lawless mean fellow." Hendrick shook his head.

"He's nothing but a clown; an unimportant lewd person you must pay no attention to." Dee told him. "It is no secret that they all despise me."

Sending several looks to those peering at them soon brought peace.

Dee attracted the attention of the musicians in the corner.

"Give us a recital? Certainly!" The leader instructed his players to begin playing merrily.

Nothing could be heard over the music of stringed instruments, which was how Dee liked it.

## 9.

"It is a step in the right direction." Hendrick agreed.

"Stop transgressing." Dee told him. "With a swirl of a feather your attention is gone!" He shook his head. "The empire is under threat!" Dee warned. "The information was most significant."

Shaking his head, he looked at Hendrick. "It is your job to find out the plan."

Hendrick nodded.

"I shall protect her Majesty." Dee told him, and disappeared.

"Such strange ocurrences, whatever is going on at the Palace?" The crowd asked.

The coat of arms above the door was bold and of red. The hubbub reached the receiving hall where Dee was explaining. "The danger is increasing, her Majesty must be informed." Dee insisted. "She will be safe with an armed escort at twilight, when cocks and hens go to roost."

The order came: "Advance the plan!"

"Such a plan is not convenient," her Majesty began, following the man as he took the winding passages in the Palace cellars to the secret hideaway.

The chant rose. "The Palace shall be conquered."

He tripped on the path's projecting corner stone, stumbled and caught himself. Hugging the wall corner so as not to be seen as he approached the brook, Hendrick hid behind a crumbled wall, listening.

"Everything was set in array, but I shall not be befooled." Hendrick said to himself. "I shall not rush impetuously."

He thought to himself: "This is a terrible chance to take." He shook his head. "I hope I will never be called on it."

Then, he heard their leader speak. "When I give the command, you will leap into action without delay."

Hendrick's eyes widened. He hadn't believed the plan until then.


"Who is here making enquiries?" Dee frowned.

"It is I, regarding the Queen."

There was a pause between the two men.

"It is a trick. It is him who wishes her Majesty harm!" One man declared, pointing at Dee.

Shaking his head, Dee sighed. "I would never and I do not weet the plan to take in the Palace."

"We will make him confess." A Palace guard said.

Dee muttered under his breath.

"He's using some kind of code. He's using discreet language." They exclaimed.

"Moderate your tone." Dee told him.

Silence fell.

## 10.

"What happened?" The nightwatchman asked.

The tavern owner spoke. "They say he is nothing but an unrefined thief, paying with a counterfeit cheque!"

"He is a thief." The other man shook his head, waving his knife at the accused.

"Sheath your knife or I shall have you set up for an arrest." The nightwatchman said.

The arresting officer took charge from the nightwatchman, threatening the thief with instruments of torture and the torture device for pinching fingers before the magistrate would send him to the hangman.

"The charge is theft. I will only need to attend here every recurring four days." The thief sneered.

He received a slap around the head to quieten him.

"Is there a reward?" The nightwatchman was asked: he laughed.

# 11.

The group was active here, that was obvious. Hendrick hid when he saw three men approach.

"Oppose to belief, this is a mere token." One man said.

The instruction came then: "You must break the stone."

"That is challenging." One man sighed.

"Break it? We must destroy it." The first voice replied.

It was daubed with dirt to hide it. Hendrick watched from his hiding place.

"We must construe the truth. And not cheat." The first man said.

"It will counterpoise." Another shook his head.

"It is a matter of the utmost urgency." The first man urged. "There is no surplus. Do it!"

Once the group had gone, Hendrick dug up the stone, seeing several symbols on it that he recognised. He knew then he had to take it to show Dr Dee and Katherine.

## 12.

The stuffed head of a stag in one corner watched everyone in the room. They all wore high shoes and a high crowned hat, and a ruff. In Winter, their hats and gloves of kid leather kept them warm.

"It is your job to serve the guests." The servant was told.

A servant stacked firewood by the fireplace before shaking the table linen over the table before the guests arrived for dinner.

Serving the meal, he couldn't help but overhear the conversations.

"There have been several grave incidents." The master of the house paused for effect. "The gardens are fenced, for security."

The men shook their heads in disgust. "Amongst them, we must have mealed." One man shuddered.

Their meal passed pleasantly.

"Have a night cap (drink) before you leave." They were bade.

Not one of them failed to enjoy the night cap, he saw.

## 13.

In Dee's lab, Hendrick laid the stone on the table for him and Katherine to examine: they took it to another room.

It was then he saw the papers on time travel and wormholes although he did not understand them. They were half under the working that Dr Dee called a calendar. It was another great work that Hendrick did not understand.

When Dr Dee returns, he is reading the papers.

"You are a deceitful, foolish stupid person." Dee told him, angry.

Hendrick's expression was lamentable and he was afraid. "I am most sorrowful for my misgivings."

Hesitating, Dee accepts his apology.

"I want to learn more." Hendrick whispered.

Dee showed him extracts in his diary then, telling tales of defiance and brave deeds from lands far away.

"My stay with the geographer, Gerardus Mercator, was more than a way to pass the time. He produced an atlas, a book with maps from all over the world. Such an accomplishment."

Hendrick nodded.

"He gave me a present of the brass staff and globes." Dee pointed to the items.

"The communication crystal from Uriel the angel is an object of wonder." Hendrick said then.

Dee nodded wisely.

"After the incidents of a new star and a comet, my knowledge helped Queen Elizabeth to build a great Navy under Drake. They had subtle questions and suggestions but were willing to work together."

"What other complements have you made?" Hendrick asked after a while.

Dee smiled. "I agreed to help James Burbage in the building of the Theatre. After his death, his sons had to dissemble the building by night and rebuilt it as the Globe in Southwark."

Hendrick's mouth dropped open in shock.

"In the future, there will be no need for a small boat used for river crossings, there will be a tunnel under the Thames." Dee told him, smiling at his shock. "I can name beforehand the future."

"What else will happen in the future?" Hendrick asked.

"Many significant finds." Dee said.

"And?"

"The words of the supernatural will be quickly forbidden." Dee shook his head.

A thought struck Hendrick. "Will you be able to travel to the future?"

Dee nodded wisely.

Hendrick stared at him in amazement.

## Part 3 is written in both languages

# 1.

Outside, the ward watchman strode by, walking his route up to the port and back again.

Outside, the ward (one of the 26 areas into which the City of London is divided for local administration) watchman (parish officer appointed to patrol the streets by night) strode by, walking his route up to the City gate and back again.

The foister, the nipper and their shadows skirted the pools of dark, biding their time.

The pickpocket, the cutpurse and their accomplices who identify and distract victims skirted the pools of dark, biding their time.

Hendrick looked around, seeing faces that he didn't recognise and some that he did, realising that most of the drinkers in the tavern knew each other. Eavesdropping, Hendrick was drawn in.

Hendrick looked around, seeing faces that he didn't recognise and some that he did, realising that most of the drinkers in the tavern knew each other. Eavesdropping, Hendrick was drawn in.

"Dee is a villian, thrasonical and a sot." Arthur declared.

"Dee is a low born man, boastful and a fool." Arthur declared.

"He is Termagant." Nicholas nodded.

"He is Termagant (a ranting character in old plays)." Nicholas nodded.

"He is yaw, yet he acts indifferent and is lewd." Thomas agreed.

"He is out of control, yet he acts ordinary and ignorant." Thomas agreed.

"I heard he is a swinge-buckler, and a Setebos." Rupert whispered not so quietly.

"I heard he is a bully, and a Setebos (the name of a fiend)." Rupert whispered not so quietly.

"It is known that he is a skilless spial." They all agreed.

"It is known that he is an ignorant spy." They all agreed.

"Dee is spirited since Kelley left." Thomas whispered then.

"Dee is haunted since Kelley left." Thomas whispered then.

"Don't be shrewd and scathful." Hendrick scolded. "Dr Dee is an audacious bawcock."

"Don't be mischievous and destructive." Hendrick scolded. "Dr Dee is a daring, fine fellow."

"You are a single ninny." Lionel said, pointing at Hendrick.

"You are a feeble fool." Lionel said, pointing at Hendrick.

"He is a rook; a revolt; a rack of a man, nothing but a rag." Rupert spat.

"He is a cheater, a rebel; a wreck of a man, nothing but a rag (term of contempt)." Rupert spat.

"He is a prime patch." Arthur sneered.

"He is a lecherous, mean fellow." Arthur sneered.

"Like Ouphe, you are pardous but a motley-minded mome." Thomas said to Hendrick.

"Like Ouphe (a fairy), you are perilously keen but a foolish stupid person." Thomas said to Hendrick.

"Your mind is perdu with tales of the fanatical." Rupert agreed.

"Your mind is lost with tales of the fanatical." Rupert agreed.

"You act greenly, you exsufficate dullard." Hendrick replied.

"You act foolishly, you contemptible dull person." Hendrick replied.

"You are nothing but a cowish geck in daub." Arthur declared.

"You are nothing but a cowardly fool in disguise." Arthur declared.

"You are a capocchia." Hendrick replied.

"You are a simpleton." Hendrick replied.

"You are a caitiff of his, taken over by a bug; a bavin, just like the antick." He was told.

"You are a captive of his, taken over by a spectre; worthless, just like the fool in old plays." He was told.

"He is a cozener, nothing but a quat." Lionel agreed.

"He is a confidence trickster, nothing but a pimple." Lionel agreed.

"He tries to be the approver, but he is a zany." Thomas pointed out.

"He tries to be the one who proves, but he is a clown." Thomas pointed out.

"Dr Dee is an inkhorn-mate, that is all." Hendrick shook his head.

"Dr Dee is a man of learning and hated for it, that is all." Hendrick shook his head.

"Mephistophilus delivers instructions to him directly." Lionel whispered.

"Mephistophilus (the name of a familiar spirit) delivers instructions to him directly." Lionel whispered.

"They say he is an anthropophaginian." Arthur added.

"They say he is a cannibal." Arthur added.

"He is a chamberer, a Popinjay." Lionel declared.

"He is an effeminate man, a conceited overly fashionable man." Lionel declared.

Rupert laughed. "So it is seated. He is a roisting, roynish, rubious rook!"

Rupert laughed. "So it is confirmed. He is a violent, mangy, ruddy cheater!"

"You are nothing but a revolt; a ripe revolt." Hendrick shook his head.

"You are nothing but a rebel; a drunk rebel." Hendrick shook his head.

Another man joined in. "He is diffused and dearn."

Another man joined in. "He is confused and lonely."

Hendrick smiled at him, glad to have an ally.

Hendrick smiled at him, glad to have an ally.

"No, he is a facinorous espial." Arthur argued.

"No, he is a wicked spy." Arthur argued.

"You are a braid cracker." Hendrick was told.

"You are a deceitful boaster." Hendrick was told.

Hendrick replied. "You are a lither loon."

Hendrick replied. "You are a lazy low contemptible fellow."

"You are a meazel." Another man agreed, on Hendrick's side.

"You are a mean person." Another man agreed, on Hendrick's side.

"You are a lag." Rupert replied.

"You are the lowest of people." Rupert replied.

Shaking his head, Hendrick got up from the table, walking across the room away from them all.

Shaking his head, Hendrick got up from the table, walking across the room away from them all.

Rupert followed, stopping him. "You are forbode to use the jakes."

Rupert followed, stopping him. "You are forbidden to use the privy."

In response, Hendrick pushed him out of the way.

In response, Hendrick pushed him out of the way.

Rupert snarled. "That will cost you lief."

Rupert snarled. "That will cost you dear."

"A bung of lowre and you think you rule all!" One cried.

"A pocket of coin and you think you rule all!" One cried.

"Via!" Rupert shouted, consumed with yellowness.

"Off with you!" Rupert shouted, consumed with jealousy.

Hendrick didn't move.

Hendrick didn't move.

"You are a beshrew!" Rupert screamed at him, holding the poniard level with Hendrick's face.

"You are an evil befal!" Rupert screamed at him, holding the dagger level with Hendrick's face.

A flash of light caught the poinard as Rupert moved.

A flash of light caught the dagger as Rupert moved.

The whoo-bub fell whist whiles...

The hubbub fell silent until...

"What betid!" The ward watchman asked, hurrying into the tavern.

"What happened!" The officer asked, hurrying into the tavern.

"There has been a grave occurent." Lionel told him.

"There has been a grave incident." Lionel told him.

"He's a serpent." Thomas claimed.

"He's a worm." Thomas claimed.

"What is this wroth?" The ward watchman boomed.

"What is this calamity?" The officer boomed.

Silence fell.

Silence fell.

"Am I yare?" He asked.

"Am I being understood?" He asked.

They nodded, yarely, telling of the threats to stain him, which Hendrick ignored and how Hendrick was refusing to subscribe. The man with the poniard was very mistempered, and heady. They were gast, the eyewitnesses reported.

They nodded, readily, telling of the threats to disfigure him, which Hendrick ignored and how Hendrick was refusing to succumb. The man with the dagger was very angry, and violent. They were frightened, the eyewitnesses reported.

The watchman summoned the arch leech to tend to Hendrick's injuries, arresting Rupert and leaving the tavern with him.

The watchman summoned the chief physician to tend to Hendrick's injuries, arresting Rupert and leaving the tavern with him.

The arch leech, sprag and point-de-vice, is an importing cavalero, commanding respect everywhere he went. Silence fell as he entered the tavern.

The chief physician, quick and faultless, is a significant gentleman, commanding respect everywhere he went. Silence fell as he entered the tavern.

"He is bisson." The arch leech concluded to the crowd. "He must be allowed to recure." He advised, turning his attention to Hendrick.

"He is blind." The chief physician concluded to the crowd. "He must be allowed to recover." He advised, turning his attention to Hendrick.

"What is the tarriance? Act festinately. The pain is fineless." Hendrick groaned.

"What is the delay? Act quickly. The pain is endless." Hendrick groaned.

Have coragio, he was told.

Have courage, he was told.

He struggled to suspire his threne of thought. His expression uneath concealed his teen, his tire shading his face.

He struggled to breathe his lament of grief. His expression hardly concealed his grief, his head dress (attire) shading his face.

The skin had to be pieled before the neeld could be inserted. Hendrick passed out.

The skin had to be shaven before the needle could be inserted. Hendrick passed out.

## 2.

The stranger tried to blend in, becoming a street higgler. From there, he watched – everything and everyone. There were plenty of artificers – a cozier, a costermonger, a currier and a cordwainer - in the vicinity. His expression was wailful. It was obvious he was voluble and of sufferance, his eyes holding a hidden wannion.

The foreigner tried to blend in, becoming a street peddlar. From there, he watched – everything and everyone. There were plenty of skilled workmen – a tailor, a stall holder (especially selling fruit), a craftsman who turns skins into leather and a worker in the best leather - in the vicinity. His expression was lamentable. It was obvious he was fickle and suffering, his eyes holding a hidden vengence.

Dr Dee knew of him, and knew that he would be the one to tell him where to find Hendrick.

Dr Dee knew of him, and knew that he would be the one to tell him where to find Hendrick.

Having found Hendrick easily, Dee put his plan into action.

Having found Hendrick easily, Dee put his plan into action.

His actions would be successive because he was parted and parlous, and Dr Dee was orgulous of him.

His actions would be succeeding because he was gifted and shrewd, and Dr Dee was proud of him.

Hendrick was rapt. He was filled with a palmy pudency: Dr Dee was orgulous of him.

Hendrick was transported with emotion. He was filled with a victorious modesty: Dr Dee was proud of him.

With praise ringing in his ears, Hendrick's mouth fell open when Dr Dee offered him a position as his assistant. He agreed quickly.

With praise ringing in his ears, Hendrick's mouth fell open when Dr Dee offered him a position as his assistant. He agreed quickly.

By averring the agreement, there was nothing to baccare, Hendrick knew.

By confirming the agreement, there was nothing to keep back, Hendrick knew.

Dee was fain his new assistant was forgetive and not exsufficate, as he was forspent. There would be no sense of emulation. He was in dich, yet distempered, distraught - and dry. He led his assistant to the tavern.

Diffused, Hendrick followed, demurely desperate to have his master like him.

Dee was glad his new assistant was inventive and not contemptible, as he was exhausted. There would be no sense of jealousy. He was in an optative mood, yet discontented, distracted - and thirsty. He led his assistant to the tavern.

Confused, Hendrick followed, solemnly determined to have his master like him.

Looking around, Hendrick concluded there was a sense of capricious, a constant sense of complexion with a hint of cautel. Nobody inside was cautelous, just buxom with an audacious streak, tossing their statute-caps in the air in celebration.

Looking around, Hendrick concluded there was a sense of lascivious, a determined sense of passion with a hint of deceit. Nobody inside was insidious, just obedient with a spirited streak, tossing their woollen caps in the air in celebration.

He heard snatches of conversation:

He heard snatches of conversation:

"She is a no good gamester."

"She is a no good frolicsome person, a loose woman."

"He is nayward, he cannot be swayed."

"He is towards denial, he cannot be swayed."

"I do not wish to baffle you."

"I do not wish to embarrass you."

"He took in snuff straight."

"He took offence immediately."

Dee dropped his voice. "We must be alone to expostulate." However, he saw the questions in Hendrick's face, and encouraged him to speak.

Dee dropped his voice. "We must be alone to discuss." (to expostulate is to set forth or state in detail - ie to expound theories. or to explain.) However, he saw the questions in Hendrick's face, and encouraged him to speak.

"This is an agreement of commodity." Hendrick said airily. "I am not franked and I am treated as more of a feere than a feeder."

"This is an agreement of convenience." Hendrick said airily. "I am not confined and I am treated as more of a companion than a servant."

Dee nodded. "Agreed."

Dee nodded. "Agreed."

## 3.

Hendrick tried to take in everything in Dee's lab, knowing that everything had an important purpose. In the corner stood a statua of unknown, and a state by a large sanded vase.

Hendrick tried to take in everything in Dee's lab, knowing that everything had an important purpose. In the corner stood a statue of unknown, and a canopied chair by a large vase marked with yellow spots.

On the table amongst the horologe, unravalled inkle, the gad lay beside the pouncet-box and periapts lay on the table beside the perspective. The box was latten, unusual in it's design.

On the table amongst the clock, unravalled narrow tape, the pointed instrument lay beside the box for holding perfumes and charms worn round the neck lay on the table beside the telescope. The box was made of brass, unusual in it's design.

A pomander hung in the window, glistening in the light on a tundish, umbered but not vinewed, and a table-book. The table-book he saw was filled with strange symbols and mystical tales. Beside that, the three spheres clinquant in the light.

A perfumed ball hung in the window, glistening in the light on a funnel, stained but not mouldy, and a notebook. The notebook he saw was filled with strange symbols and mystical reckonings. Beside that, the three spheres glittered in the light.

That was all he got to see as the room shouldered into darkness, yet there was a strange legerity around the room.

That was all he got to see as the room plunged into darkness, yet there was a strange lightness around the room.

"There must be a steeled, still temperance in the room so that the material must be sheer and sere." Dee advised him. "My time must be continuate. Do not jut my space."

"There must be a set, constant temperature in the room so that the material must be dry and unmixed." Dee advised him. "My time must be uninterrupted. Do not encroach my space."

There was a pause and Hendrick wondered what was expected of him.

There was a pause and Hendrick wondered what was expected of him.

"After a long travail, the results are toward." Dee told him.

"After a long toil, the results are nearly ready." Dee told him.

Katherine argued, but Hendrick didn't catch what she said.

Katherine argued, but Hendrick didn't catch what she said.

"It is plausive. Nothing is point-de-vice." Dee told her.

"It is plausible. Nothing is faultless." Dee told her.

Hendrick nodded.

Hendrick nodded.

"It is, at the moment, only a tested theorick." Dee pointed out.

"It is, at the moment, only a pure theory." Dee pointed out.

Hendrick nodded again.

Hendrick nodded again.

Katherine spoke then. "Father, why do you need this man?" Her voice was of sneap, spoke softly. Her expression was sorriest.

Katherine spoke then. "Father, why do you need this man?" Her voice was of sarcasm, spoke gently. Her expression was most sorrowful.

"He displayed a scantling of sheen." Dee replied.

"He displayed a small portion of brilliancy." Dee replied.

"I shall not forspeak him. Your secrets will not be imbared." Hendrick promised her.

"I shall not speak against him. Your secrets will not be bared." Hendrick promised her.

His speech was sacrificial, Hendrick realised. Dee's words: "You are of skill" still were in his mind.

His speech was reverent, as words used in religious worship, Hendrick realised. Dee's words: "You are of importance" still were in his mind.

After that, he was left alone in the room with Katherine. His attention turned back to the table. Examining the smaller sphere: "There are strange denotements." Hendrick frowned.

After that, he was left alone in the room with Katherine. His attention turned back to the table.

Examining the smaller sphere: "There are strange markings." Hendrick frowned.

Katherine explained. "It has been derived from the Gods."

Katherine explained. "It has descended from the Gods."

"It is mere estimation!" Hendrick replied, his tone of bob.

"It is mere conjecture!" Hendrick replied, his tone of sarcasm.

Katherine shook her head.

Katherine shook her head.

"I do not fear being firked." Hendrick told her.

"I do not fear being severely chastised." Hendrick told her.

Amusement danced in her eyes. "You do not?"
Amusement danced in her eyes. "You do not?"
He shook his head. "Tell me more." He gestured around the room.
He shook his head. "Tell me more." He gestured around the room.

"Everything is put away feater in order to find it in a hurry, even after a long gest." Katherine informed him, stopping him as he began. "Do not temper the two potions." Placing others in front of him, Katherine ordered. "Mell these together."

"Everything is put away neatly in order to find it in a hurry, even after a long period." Katherine informed him, stopping him as he began. "Do not mix the two potions." Placing others in front of him, Katherine ordered. "Mix these together."

98

"It is quail," Hendrick frowned.
"It is languid," Hendrick frowned.

"It will fleet. Make sure it is seeled." She instructed. "Then limn and level the cuttle. Do not drumble, nor drive."

"It will float. Make sure it is closed." She instructed. "Then draw and aim the knife. Do not dwaddle, nor rush impetuously."

Frowning, she guided his shaky hands. Her touch so enthralled him, Hendrick failed to know Dee's presence.

Frowning, she guided his shaky hands. Her touch so enthralled him, Hendrick failed to acknowledge Dee's presence.

Dee saw they had an immediacy, and did not like it.

Dee saw they had a close connection, and did not like it.

"I know not who to trow." He snarled at Katherine in a rapture of rage. "It is up to you to project the young man. He cannot trow for himself."

"I know not who to trust." He snarled at Katherine in a fit of rage. "It is up to you to shape the young man. He cannot think for himself."

Hendrick glut hastily, as Dr Dee continued his rant. The words caused him to knap and Hendrick escaped to the tavern's hurly.

Hendrick swallowed hastily, as Dr Dee continued his rant. The words caused him to crack and Hendrick escaped to the tavern's noise and confusion.

*99*

Dee moved featly, gaberdine wrapped tightly around him to keep out the bitter wind, finding Hendrick in the corner of the tavern ten minutes later.

Dee moved nimbly, outer coat wrapped tightly around him to keep out the bitter wind, finding Hendrick in the corner of the tavern ten minutes later.

Looking up from his glass, Hendrick gave a regreet as Dee approached him.

Looking up from his glass, Hendrick gave a salutation as Dee approached him.

"I will allow it if you are serious about Katherine."

"I will allow it if you are serious about Katherine."

Hendrick's jaw dropped open in shock.

Hendrick's jaw dropped open in shock.

"I must be the first to gratulate her. It must not be fub off." Dee shook his head, not waiting for the answer first. "Does that fadge you?"

"I must be the first to congratulate her. It must not be put off." Dee shook his head, not waiting for the answer first. "Does that suit you?"

Hendrick tried to englut. "Yes sir."

Hendrick tried to swallow speedily. "Yes sir."

"Do not let her distaste you." He was warned.

"Do not let her corrupt you." He was warned.

He failed to glose, and was encouraged to finish his drink before returning.

He failed to comment, and was encouraged to finish his drink before returning.

Upon his return, across the room, Dee gave him a mop.

Upon his return, across the room, Dee gave him a nod.

He wafted Hendrick over. "It needs to be tempered properly before allowed to quench." He instructed. "Don't forget to rake it."

He beckoned Hendrick over. "It needs to be mixed properly before allowed to grow cool." He instructed. "Don't forget to cover it."

"Yes sir." Hendrick replied, hoping this would be enough.

"Yes sir." Hendrick replied, hoping this would be enough.

"It was rawly covered and it was frushed before." Dee explained.

"It was inadequately covered and was bruised before." Dee explained.

Dee walked across the room to leave, pausing at Katherine's side. "You are pathetical." Dee told her.

Dee walked across the room to leave, pausing at Katherine's side. "You are hypocritical." Dee told her.

His behaviour is moonish, Hendrick thought: knowing he was not allowed to glose.

His behaviour is inconstant, Hendrick thought: knowing he was not allowed to comment.

Katherine distracted him when Dee left, telling him the story of how the place was rebuilt. The fire was set in the bay, and soon took hold. It destroyed half of the library at Mortlake before it was controlled.

Katherine distracted him when Dee left, telling him the story of how the place was rebuilt. The fire was set in the space between the main timbers of the roof, and soon took hold. It destroyed half of the library at Mortlake before it was controlled.

"We feared all was perdu!" Katherine shook her head.

"We feared all was lost!" Katherine shook her head.

Hendrick nodded, feeling something was meant of him at her pause.

Hendrick nodded, feeling something was meant of him at her pause.

Katherine took a deep breath. "But there was no sense of denay, no condolement from father."

Katherine took a deep breath. "But there was no sense of denial, no grief from father."

Hendrick frowned. "Did not that fester? You should be despatched by the loss."

Hendrick frowned. "Did not that rankle? You should be bereaved by the loss."

Katherine shrugged. "It was primer that everyone escaped alive."

Katherine shrugged. "It was more important that everyone escaped alive."

In the silence, she looked at him.

In the silence, she looked at him.

"Would you like to see it?"

"Would you like to see it?"

Hendrick smiled at her, and followed her through the house, down the cranks to the library. He gasped when he saw the walls of books. Going closer, he could see that there were a lot that were written by Dr John Dee – counting, he found there were 49 in total.

Hendrick smiled at her, and followed her through the house, down the winding passages to the library. He gasped when he saw the walls of books. Going closer, he could see that there were a lot that were written by Dr John Dee – counting, he found there were 49 in total.

"Queen Mary did not like the idea of having all books, manuscripts and records in one place when it was proposed in 1556." She spread her hands. "So it is here."

"Queen Mary did not like the idea of having all books, manuscripts and records in one place when it was proposed in 1556." She spread her hands. "So it is here."

"Are there many visitors?" Hendrick asked.

"Are there many visitors?" Hendrick asked.

Katherine nodded, watching him go to the shelves of Dr Dee's books. He paused at General and Rare Memorials pertayning to the Perfect Arte of Navigation.

Katherine nodded, watching him go to the shelves of Dr Dee's books. He paused at General and Rare Memorials pertayning to the Perfect Arte of Navigation.

"Father advised Queen Elizabeth on navigation and discovery in foreign lands by the British Empery for many years. He was the one who produced the term." She had a proud look in her eyes.

"Father advised Queen Elizabeth on navigation and discovery in foreign lands by the British Empire for many years. He was the one who produced the term." She had a proud look in her eyes.

Putting the book back carefully, Hendrick then found a slimmer volume Monas Hieroglyphica. Opening it, he saw it contained lots of symbols. His frown told her that he didn't understand.

Putting the book back carefully, Hendrick then found a slimmer volume Monas Hieroglyphica. Opening it, he saw it contained lots of symbols. His frown told her that he didn't understand.

Katherine smiled at his confusion. "That one expresses the mystical unity of all creation."

Katherine smiled at his confusion. "That one expresses the mystical unity of all creation."

Quickly, Hendrick replaced it on the shelf.

Quickly, Hendrick replaced it on the shelf.

"There are many science works." Katherine pointed out De Trigono, Testamentum Johannis Dee Philosophi Summi ad Johannem Guryun Transmissum, An Account of the Manner in which a Certayn Copper-smith in the Land of Moores, and a Certayn Moore Transmuted Copper to Gold.

"There are many science works." Katherine pointed out De Trigono, Testamentum Johannis

Dee Philosophi Summi ad Johannem Guryun Transmissum, An Account of the Manner in which a Certayn Copper-smith in the Land of Moores, and a Certayn Moore Transmuted Copper to Gold.

Hendrick saw also On The Mystical Rule of the Seven Planets, True and Faithful Relation of Dr John Dee and Some Spirits by John Dee, Mysteriorum Liber Sextus et Sanctus, Compendium Heptarchiae Mysticae, De Heptarchia Mystica, Tuba Veneris... He shook his head, sure that these were above his understanding.

Hendrick saw also On The Mystical Rule of the Seven Planets, True and Faithful Relation of Dr John Dee and Some Spirits by John Dee, Mysteriorum Liber Sextus et Sanctus, Compendium Heptarchiae Mysticae, De Heptarchia Mystica, Tuba Veneris... He shook his head, sure that these were above his understanding.

"I'm sure you would find father's diary of more interest." Katherine told him. "Ask him to show you."

"I'm sure you would find father's diary of more interest." Katherine told him. "Ask him to show you."

Hendrick smiled at her then.

Hendrick smiled at her then.

## 4.

The weapon was hent as the instruction was given: Impeticos the poniard.

The weapon was seized as the instruction was given: Pocket the dagger.

However, the watchman did not have the poniard when he arrived with Rupert in front of the beak.

However, the officer did not have the dagger when he arrived with Rupert in front of the magistate.

"I am mated that you would impeach evidence." The beak told him.

"I am dismayed that you would bring into question evidence." The judge told him.

Turning to the court, he began.

Turning to the court, he began.

"It has been leged that nobody was incensed. Yet, several men told of threats from the accused to stain the victim despite his refusing to subscribe. Eyewitnesses were afeared and gast."

"It has been alleged that nobody was incited. Yet, several men told of threats from the accused to disfigure the victim despite his refusing to succumb. Eyewitnesses were afraid and frightened."

"I am sentenced to deem." Rupert moaned.

"I am sentenced to doom." Rupert moaned.

"The incident was intended to be a kindless lethe of a juvenal." The beak continued.

"The incident was intended to be an unnatural death of a young man." The magistrate continued.

Rupert muttered for forgiveness.

Rupert muttered for forgiveness.

"You are scathful and shrewd, and you seek shrift from me?" The beak shook his head.

"You are destructive and mischievous, and you seek absolution from me?" The magistrate shook his head.

"Where is your credit?" He said to the watchman.

"Where is your report?" He said to the officer.

He displayed a curstness, and read through the information. "Those candle-wasters, drunk on Charneco, talked loudly over the broken music, had an argument."

He displayed a shrewishness, and read through the information. "Those persons who sit up all night to drink, drunk on Charneco (a sweet wine), talked loudly over the music of stringed instruments, had an argument."

"He brought the poniard down with force over the man's face."

"He brought the dagger down with force over the man's face."

Rupert stuttered his apology.

Rupert stuttered his apology.

"Your apology is lated." The beak peered at him over his spectacles. "I'm sending you to the derrick."

"Your apology is belated." The magistrate peered at him over his spectacles. "I'm sending you to the hangman."

## 5.

The atmosphere was both of mood and inwardness, intentively indigest.

The atmosphere was both of anger and intimacy, attentively disordered.

Hendrick knew that he looked indifferent, compared to Katherine - she was quaint. It was obvious she was not unbreathed.

Hendrick knew that he looked ordinary, compared to Katherine - she was curiously beautiful. It was obvious she was not unpracticed.

Being fulsome made him emulous. He was flush and fancy-free. He gave oeilliad across to her...

Being lustful made him jealous. He was full of vigour and untouched by love. He gave an amorous glance across to her...

It would be easier if she was sightless, he thought.

It would be easier if she was unsightly, he thought.

"I wouldn't want you to misthink of me." He said to her.

"I wouldn't want you to think ill of me." He said to her.

Her answer was mobled, but he heard it. "Find another way to fleet."

Her answer was muffled, but he heard it. "Find another way to pass the time."

She attended to the vegetives; she was tight and yet stark, her expression tempered.

She attended to the herbs; she was stiff and yet nimble, her expression mixed.

The conversation ended there. Silence fell for an hour until dinner.

The conversation ended there. Silence fell for an hour until dinner.

"If I can make a prompture. We should capitulate." He looked at her longly as she served their food.

"If I can make a suggestion. We should work together." He looked at her longingly as she served their food.

"This is nothing but a drollery." She gave scall. "Here is your dole, and your pottage."

"This is nothing but a puppet show." She gave a word of reproach. "Here is your free allowance of bread, and your stew."

He was ravin, watching as she stooped to beteem the ale and sat beside him. Cutting a moiety of pie for afterwards. A tiny shive only.

He was ravenous, watching as she stooped to pour out the ale and sat beside him. Cutting a portion of pie for afterwards. A tiny slice only.

"We shall convive." She declared.

"We shall feast together." She declared.

He sighed inly. The lush meal was fit for a King.

He sighed inwardly. The luxuriant meal was fit for a King.

His permanent defeature made him recognisable everywhere he went. But his refined yet bushy beard entranced her. Her beautiful long hair was cain-coloured, her skin delicately pale. She knew

*109*

men desired her. As he sneaped her bottom, it was obvious Hendrick was not oblivious to her charms.
His permanent disfigurement made him recognisable everywhere he went. But his bolted yet bushy beard entranced her. Her beautiful long hair was red coloured, her skin delicately pale. She knew men desired her. As he pinched her bottom, it was obvious Hendrick was not oblivious to her charms.

He gave her a largess, a medal. Wooing her with words pleached with romanticism. Soon they were joined in couplement.

He gave her a present, a portrait in a locket. Wooing her with words interwoven with romanticism. Soon they were joined in union.

The jar was the first thing he was aware of.
The ticking of the clock was the first thing he was aware of.
"This should never be divulged." She warned.
"This should never be spoken of." She warned.
"You have an extent of fact." He smiled.
"You have a seizure of guilt." He smiled.
She scowled.
She scowled.
"It was a quiddit, not a quip!" He explained.
"It was a subtle question, not a taunt!" He explained.
"I find it an unnecessary taxing."
"I find it an unnecessary satire."

She crossed the room to the boitier vert, extracting from within the medal. There was no time to tender him and her feelings as there came a timeless knock. Wrapping the velure around her, she disappeared.

She crossed the room to the green box, extracting from within the portrait in a locket. There was no time to have consideration for him and her feelings, as there came an untimely knock. Wrapping the velvet around her, she disappeared.

An hour later, she was forced to consort him to the wherry. "If that was to claw me,"

An hour later, she was forced to accompany him to the small river crossing boat. "If that was to flatter me,"

"I only meant to atone." He looked at her agazed.

"I only meant to put people at one." He looked at her in amazement.

Katherine nodded. "The password is: The Thames looks bollen today. You should reply: He arrived anight, he did not see."

Katherine nodded. "The password is: The Thames looks swollen today. You should reply: He arrived by night, he did not see."

Hendrick nodded, memorising the phrases as an argument broke out in the street below.

Hendrick nodded, memorising the phrases as an argument broke out in the street below.

"It was but a bruit!"

"It was but a rumour!"

"You are the bawd!"

"You are the procurer!"

The two men had hold of each other then.

The two men had hold of each other then.

"You have a chance to approve." She told him, drawing his attention back to her.

"You have a chance to make good." She told him, drawing his attention back to her.

"I shall not forspeak him. I am in his depend." He reassured her. He stooped to inclip her. Even touching her tarred him. "Good-den," he tipped his hat to her, before leaving.

"I shall not speak against him. I am in his service." He reassured her. He stooped to embrace her. Even touching her excited him. "Good evening," he tipped his hat to her, before leaving.

His tone caused her to quake.

His tone caused her to tremble.

"It was my intention only to possess you." She whispered.

"It was my intention only to inform you." She whispered.

He took his seat on the wherry, smiling at her. "And I, you." Hendrick replied.

He took his seat on the small boat, smiling at her. "And I, you." Hendrick replied.

She quailed.

She fainted.

## 6.

London's best playwrights were all mewed up in the room. But there was no abhor until a brabble erupted amongst those in the room.

London's best playwrights were all confined in the room. But there was no protest until a quarrel erupted amongst those in the room.

Augustus saw Humphrey admiring his reflection. "A sign of vainness in man means that he has a vailing validity."

Augustus saw Humphrey admiring his reflection. "A sign of vanity in man means that he has a lowering value."

"Sith your speech is skimble-skamble, he is tilly-vally!" Humphrey replied.

"Since your speech is rambling, he is tilly-vally!" (an exclamation of contempt.) Humphrey replied.

Laughter.

Laughter.

"Such a verbal man should be a scholar." William suggested.

"Such a wordy man should be a scholar." William suggested.

"Are you unpregnant?" Humphrey turned to him.

"Are you stupid?" Humphrey turned to him.

"You would take up?" Leopold asked Humphrey.

"You would make up a quarrel?" Leopold asked Humphrey.

"You are a troublesome squarer!" Humphrey replied.

"You are a troublesome quarreller!" Humphrey replied.

"You are a fardel!" Augustus told him.

"You are a burden!" Augustus told him.

More laughter.

More laughter.

Ernest came into the room then. "What is this garboil?" He demanded.

Ernest came into the room then. "What is this disorder?" He demanded.

Silence fell.

Silence fell.

"I have a specially for you," he said to the playwrights. Ernest went on to explain, finishing the plan with: "It is a vastidity, a vast. It vaunt anything done before." He looked around the group.

"I have a special contract for you," he said to the playwrights. Ernest went on to explain, finishing the plan with: "It is an immensity, a gulf. It precedes anything done before." He looked around the group.

"I intend to defy it." Leopold shouted.

"I intend to renounce it!" Leopold shouted.

"Were you previously under-wrought?" Augustus asked him.

"Were you previously undermined?" Augustus asked him.

"I intend to demerit." William murmured.

"I intend to desert." William murmured.

"Are you unquestionable?" Augustus asked William.

"Are you not inquisitive?" Augustus asked William.
William shook his head, slipping out of the room as another brabble broke out.
William shook his head, slipping out of the room as another quarrel broke out.

"Do as you are seen, or your reputation will be forever smirched. No speed for you!" They were warned.

"Do as you are instructed, or your reputation will be forever soiled. No fortune for you!" They were warned.

"It is too too tasking." Leopold shook his head.

"It is excessively challenging." Leopold shook his head.

The mood around the room was convinced.
The mood around the room was subdued.

"Convert your thinking." Ernest snapped at the playwrights.

"Change your thinking." Ernest snapped at the playwrights.

"You must cony-catch in order to colt the man." They were told.

"You must cheat in order to befool the man." They were told.

"Remember the lines of the play need to be con." He ordered.

"Remember the lines of the play need to be learnt by heart." He ordered.

"We have been conned." Leopold shook his head sadly.

"We have been deceived." Leopold shook his head sadly.

"Grave your fears." Ernest ordered. "Do not ban. In cope, you shall receive gimmal." He offered.

"Bury your fears." Ernest ordered. "Do not curse. In return, you shall receive double." He offered.

"Do not harry me or it will hack." Leopold tried.

"Do not harrass me or it will become common." Leopold tried.

"You dare me?" Ernest asked dangerously. "Via!"

"You challenge me?" Ernest asked dangerously. "Off with you!"

"How about you?" Ernest looked at Humphrey and Augustus.

"How about you?" Ernest looked at Humphrey and Augustus.

"No sir. I am in your depend." They responded meekly as Leopold left.

"No sir. I am in your service." They responded meekly as Leopold left.

"To determine, I will design of relevance. You must not doff signing." Ernest instructed.

"To conclude, I will draw up articles of relevance. You must not put off signing." Ernest instructed.

"I shall forbid the plan and I shall take the detect for setting everything in darraign." The statement read that each man had to sign.

"I shall defend the plan and I shall take the blame for setting everything in array." The statement read that each man had to sign.

"It is distaste." Humphrey whispered to Augustus.

116

"It is corrupt." Humphrey whispered to Augustus.

"His behaviour was falsing." Augustus moaned, his expression was lumpish.

"His behaviour was deceptive." Augustus moaned, his expression was dejected.

"The Master of the Revels has to agree." Humphrey reminded him.

"The Master of the Revels has to agree. (organizer of royal entertainments and official censor.)" Humphrey reminded him.

"The plan is kam." Augustus shook his head.

"The plan is crooked." Augustus shook his head.

"That is a fig!" Ernest shook his head.

"That is an insult!" Ernest shook his head.

"Don't be so judicious. The benefits countervail..." Humphrey began.

"Don't be so critical. The benefits outweigh..." Humphrey began.

He was cut off. "My reputation will be collied."

He was cut off. "My reputation will be blackened."

"It is our co-mart." Ernest said, his eyes glinting dangerously.

"It is our joint bargain." Ernest said, his eyes glinting dangerously.

"I am contrary," Augustus began. "How shall we convey?"

"I am opposed," Augustus began. "How shall we manage?"

"Do not examine the plan." They were warned. "Your job is to propagate this onto others. Do not bodge it."

"Do not question the plan." They were warned. "Your job is to forward this onto others. Do not botch it."

Silence fell.

Silence fell.

Ernest reminded them as he got up to leave. "You signed the book, you are bound by its terms. It is bootless to argue."

Ernest reminded them as he got up to leave. "You signed the papers of conditions, you are bound by its terms. It is useless to argue."

# 7.

Augustus's and Humphrey's opinions hurtled as they created the abridgement between them. So each man wrote his own and agreed the scripts parcelled would be merged to form the play.
Augustus's and Humphrey's opinions clashed as they created the short play between them. So each man wrote his own and agreed that the scripts belonging to individuals would be merged to form the play.
Ernest did not let them leave the building until it was finished.
Ernest did not let them leave the building until it was finished.
 - 'The sky was nighted...'
- 'The sky was black as night...'
- 'As night-rule...'
- 'As nightly solemnity...'
Pen down, Humphrey crossed his arms in front of his chest. "I shall not forspeak Dee." He shook his head.
Pen down, Humphrey crossed his arms in front of his chest. "I shall not speak against Dee." He shook his head.
 "You agreed to holp. You did impeticos the money. Do not cause a foreslow." Augustus told him.
 "You agreed to help. You did pocket the money. Do not cause a delay." Augustus told him.
They both sighed.
They both sighed.

"We shall impawn." Humphrey said after a moment. "I misdoubt there will be no indenting."

"We shall compromise." Humphrey said after a moment. "I suspect there will be no bargaining."

Augustus glut hastily, nodding: "He jades us."

Augustus swallowed hastily, nodding: "He treats us with contempt."

"That does not matter as long as we are paid. And released." Humphrey pointed out. "He will be indited, not us." He continued.

"That does not matter as long as we are paid. And released." Humphrey pointed out. "He will be convicted, not us." He continued.

"Nothing has been impeached. Nobody knows we are missing." Augustus pointed out.

"Nothing has been brought into question. Nobody knows we are missing." Augustus pointed out.

- "Look at them. Jauncing and jetting on the stage!" Dee loffed.

- "Look at them. Prancing and strutting on the stage!" Dee laughed.

"You should not loffe nor glose." He was told, before being dragged outside.

"You should not laugh nor comment." He was told, before being dragged outside.

"You cannot renege me of my right!" Dee cried out.

"You cannot deny me of my right." Dee cried out.

"You should not repugn." He was told.

"You should not resist." He was told.

"I did not ask for your rate." Dee retorted.

"I did not ask for your opinion." Dee retorted.

The man tried another way. "Let's propose that you were asked to…"

The man tried another way. "Let's say for the sake of argument that you were asked to…"

Dee cut him off. "I wouldn't propose anything if I were you."

Dee cut him off. "I wouldn't suppose anything if I were you."

The man slapped Dee's cheek hard. "You need to limn the map of the Palace. Do not dare to refell."

The man slapped Dee's cheek hard. "You need to draw the map of the Palace. Do not dare to refute."

Dee did as he was bade, writing down the ways in and out of the main gate beside the map.

Dee did as he was bade, writing down the ways in and out of the main gate beside the map.

"Is he telling the truth?" One asked.

"Is he telling the truth?" One asked.

"He swore a marry trap to tell the truth." Came the reply.

"He swore an oath to tell the truth." Came the reply.

"He is too green to use his invention." Came another reply.

"He is too immature to use his imagination." Came another reply.

The man shook his head. "A tale of hardiment, but lies, all lies. Hence, Dee shall be known as horn-mad and under my hest. He shall be tried and punished - he shall be drowned in an ice-brook and sent to an eterne hell."

121

The man shook his head. "A tale of defiance and brave deeds, but lies, all lies. Henceforth, Dee shall be known as brain-mad and under my command. He shall be tried and punished - he shall be drowned in an icy cold brook and sent to an eternal hell."

Scene at the Palace.
Scene at the Palace.

He tried to scan the papers but the writing was impossible to cipher.

He tried to examine subtly the papers, but the writing was impossible to decipher.

"Scant the details!" The man was furious. "Why did you propose with him?"

"Spare the details!" The man was furious. "Why did you converse with him?"

"I was forced to consign." Dee said meekly. "I could not renege the deal."

"I was forced to sign a common bond." Dee said meekly. "I could not renounce the deal."

"It is not simular?"

"It is not feigned?"

Dee shook his head. "The price on her head is rated at more than gimmal."

Dee shook his head. "The price on her head is valued at more than double."

"So, it was included...?" The question hung in the air.

"So, it was concluded...?" The question hung in the air.

"The Queen must fall." Dee's words were uttered through clenched teeth. He shook his head. "Language must be qualified. The palabras will be paid." He stared sans remorse, although his ostentation was normal.

"The Queen must fall." Dee's words were uttered through clenched teeth. He shook his head. "Language must be moderated. The words will be punished." He stared without pity, although his appearance was normal.

"It was a ratolorum; a practise that nobody dared question." He eyed Dee. "You give no hint, no thought!"

"It was a ludicrous mistake; a wicked stratagem that nobody dared question." He eyed Dee. "You give no suggestion, no thought!"

"I am but the missive. If the fault is mine, I will be shent." Dee told him.

"I am but the messenger. If the fault is mine, I will be rebuked." Dee told him.

He, mammering, thought for a while before eating the marchpanes in silence. A mess of men, who didn't like to deal with the metaphysical. Their actions were meacock, but full of mallecho. The man angled his head. "Forgive my misprision. You must display the utmost hugger-mugger about this."

He, hesitating, thought for a while before eating the sweet biscuits in silence. A company of four men, who didn't like to deal with the supernatural. Their actions were cowardly, but full of mischief. The man angled his head. "Forgive my mistake. You must display the utmost secrecy about this."

"We have to unclew this." Dee ordered.

"We have to undo this." Dee ordered.

"Your thoughts are immoment." He snapped.

"Your thoughts are unimportant." He snapped.

Dee smiled. "The detail is incony and intrinse. But it is a gimmor. I will wreak this."

Dee smiled. "The detail was fine, delicate and intricate. But it is a contrivance. I will avenge this."

- There was an interruption to the play then, a loud noise.

- There was an interruption to the play then, a loud noise.

The loud noise was a rift in the scaffoldage.

The loud noise was a split in the gallery of a theatre.

"You have gain-givings?" The main player said to the groundlings, who ran out as one.

"You have misgivings?" The main player said to the groundlings (those who sit in the pit of a theatre), who ran out as one.

"Yes!" They screamed.

"Yes!" They screamed.

Within minutes, the fire confounded the theatre. The men of the fire service were warned to the burning theatre. They completed a rigol around the fire, prest and waiting. Alas, it was a planched structure and all of the polled wood was seared.

Within minutes, the fire consumed the theatre. The men of the fire service were summoned to the burning theatre. They completed a circle around the fire, ready and waiting. Alas, it was a structure made of boards and all of the bare wood was scorched or withered.

"It is composed. The theatre shall be cogged." The head firemarshall said to the mayor.

"It is agreed. The theatre shall be dissembled." The head firemarshall said to the mayor.

"Show some expedience!" He barked at his men.

"Show some expedition (haste)!" He barked at his men.

Rumour of Dee setting a curse upon the theatre.
Rumour of Dee setting a curse upon the theatre.

"No provision had been made by Dee." He was told.

"No forecast had been made by Dee." He was told.

"Nonetheless, the plan, it is expiate." Came the reply.

"Nonetheless, the plan, it is complete." Came the reply.

In the silence, his shout of esperance echoed in the enemies ears.

In the silence, his war cry echoed in the enemies ears.

"It is typical of Dee's chare." One man shook his head.

"It is typical of Dee's turn of work." One man shook his head.

"His reputation will be latched." One man pointed out.

"His reputation will be smeared." One man pointed out.

One whispered. "He was famous for his ability to prenominate."

One whispered. "He was famous for his ability to prophesy."

"Was." One man snorted. "Not anymore."

"Was." One man snorted. "Not anymore."

He had to sowl Dee's unconscious body through the building, making sure the chains were sperred tightly before he was potched over the outer wall and left to hang.

He had to drag Dee's unconscious body through the building, making sure the chains were fastened tightly before he was pushed violently over the wall and left to hang.

"Quicken now." He snarled, laughing.

"Come to life now." He snarled, laughing.

He nicked the plan. "He cannot be killed. He will reduce secrets from the dead."

He branded with folly the plan. "He cannot be killed. He will bring back secrets from the dead."

"He created a nick and will accite the Devil."

"He tried to create a reckoning and will summon the Devil."

The men gleeked.

The men scoffed.

"Do not gleek." They were lectured.

"Do not scoff." They were lectured.

"This is set up to gallow us." He shook his head.

"This is set up to scare us." He shook his head.

"I had prevented something like this. I shall quote this."

"I had anticipated something like this. I shall note this."

Another man shook his head. "I will take no part in such patchery."

Another man shook his head. "I will take no part in such trickery."

"I will let God deliver the rate." One man agreed.

"I will let God deliver the judgement." One man agreed.

"He is forever making a prophesy or a religious rite." One man shuddered. "The strange events are of moe."

"He is forever making a calculate or a ceremony." One man shuddered. "The strange events are of frequent occurrence."

"I hear Dee spends his time in laystalls and stews." One man confessed in a whisper.

"I hear Dee spends his time in dung heaps and brothels." One man confessed in a whisper.

"It is eld. Soon he will be derogate to beg and take up."

"It is old age. Soon he will be degraded to beg and borrow money."

"He shall be damned. Send him to Bedlam!" Rose the chant.

"He shall be condemned. Send him to Bedlam! (Bedlam - Bethlehem Hospital for the deranged.)" Rose the chant.

A missive arrived.    "He is amort. It has been erewhile they did grave him."
A messenger arrived. "He is dead. It has been a short time since they did bury him."
Silence fell.
Silence fell.
- End of play
- End of play

Ernest was, overall, pleased with the work, and released Augustus and Humphrey, who ran into the daylight as if they hadn't seen it before.
Ernest was, overall, pleased with the work, and released Augustus and Humphrey, who ran into the daylight as if they hadn't seen it before.

## 8.

"Pall the barrel, and it will expulse the air harmlessly. Try to eche, it takes time to reload." Dee told him.

"Wrap the barrel and it will expel the air harmlessly. Try to eke out, it takes time to reload." Dee told him.

Hendrick nodded, and concentrated, aiming the firearm at the target as Dee had before him.

Hendrick nodded, and concentrated, aiming the firearm at the target as Dee had before him.

Katherine was present to keep nick.

Katherine was present to keep score.

The nether-stocks and a kirtle made of lockram itched. Beneath the kirtle, slops are worn, but it still itched. Hendrick tried to ignore the uncomfortable itch from his new clothes.

The stockings and a gown made of loose linen itched. Beneath the gown, loose breeches are worn, but it still itched. Hendrick tried to ignore the uncomfortable itch from his new clothes.

"Pull back the hammer. It must be factious, expedient." Dee instructed.

"Pull back the hammer. It must be instant, swift." Dee instructed.

Hendrick's hands shook so much he couldn't fire it. He lowered the firearm and shook his head.

Hendrick's hands shook so much he couldn't fire it. He lowered the firearm and shook his head.

"What happened?" Katherine asked.

"What happened?" Katherine asked.

"I failed to rive the weapon. It is my misprise." Hendrick bowed his head.

"I failed to fire the weapon. It is my mistake." Hendrick bowed his head.

In truth, he was too overwhelmed – taken into the family home, given food and money and clothing, trusted with all of Dr Dee's secrets, in relationship with his daughter. Things were going too fast.

In truth, he was too overwhelmed – taken into the family home, given food and money and clothing, trusted with all of Dr Dee's secrets, in relationship with his daughter. Things were going too fast.

"No matter." Katherine smiled at him. "Father will take you to the tavern for a drink."

"No matter." Katherine smiled at him. "Father will take you to the tavern for a drink."

Dee looked at her in shock, but nodded when Hendrick looked up at him.

Dee looked at her in shock, but nodded when Hendrick looked up at him.

At the tavern, they sat in the corner and Hendrick listened to the conversation around them.

At the tavern, they sat in the corner and Hendrick listened to the conversation around them.

"Gallow them off the scent." Came the instruction. "Sperr for the border."

"Scare them off the scent." Came the instruction. "Bolt for the border."

"It will not work, you will be reduced."

"It will not work, you will be brought back."

*130*

"His expression was mortal."

"His expression was murderous."

"It was a rash quell." One man pointed out.

"It was a violent murder." One man pointed out.

"He was of a lower ordinance, a miscreate." He shrugged.

"He was of a lower rank, an illegitimate." He shrugged.

"That doesn't make it right." He replied.

"That doesn't make it right." He replied.

"What gives you the right to censure?"

"What gives you the right to criticise?"

He refused to parle on the subject any more, noting Hendrick was listening.

He refused to talk on the subject any more, noting Hendrick was listening.

Hendrick's attention returned to Dee, noticing that everyone was looking at them then.

Hendrick's attention returned to Dee, noticing that everyone was looking at them then.

"It is unhatched, not to be unproper. We see why now. Look to welkin. It is written in the blackness of the stars." The man muttered, and moved away from them.

"It is undisclosed, not to be common to all. We see why now. Look to the sky. It is written in the blackness of the stars." The man muttered, and moved away from them.

"He is an irregulous jack." Hendrick shook his head.

"He is a lawless mean fellow." Hendrick shook his head.

"He's nothing but a lowt; an immoment lewdster you must pay no attention to." Dee told him. "It is no secret that they all misprise me."

"He's nothing but a clown; an unimportant lewd person you must pay no attention to." Dee told him. "It is no secret that they all despise me."

Sending several looks to those peering at them soon brought peace.

Sending several looks to those peering at them soon brought peace.

Dee attracted the attention of the musicians in the corner.

Dee attracted the attention of the musicians in the corner.

"Give us a cital? Certes!" The leader instructed his players to begin playing jovial.

"Give us a recital? Certainly!" The leader instructed his players to begin playing merrily.

Nothing could be heard over the broken music, which was how Dee liked it.

Nothing could be heard over the music of stringed instruments, which was how Dee liked it.

## 9.

"It is degrees in the right direction." Hendrick agreed.

"It is a step in the right direction." Hendrick agreed.

"Stop digressing." Dee told him. "With a dowle your attention is gone!" He shook his head. "The empery is under threat!" Dee warned. "The information was most importing."

"Stop transgressing." Dee told him. "With a swirl of a feather your attention is gone!" He shook his head. "The empire is under threat!" Dee warned. "The information was most significant."

Shaking his head, he looked at Hendrick. "It is your job to find out the plan."

Shaking his head, he looked at Hendrick. "It is your job to find out the plan."

Hendrick nodded.

Hendrick nodded.

"I shall protect her Majesty." Dee told him, and disappeared.

"I shall protect her Majesty." Dee told him, and disappeared.

"Such strange currents, whatever is going on at the Palace?" The crowd asked.

"Such strange occurrences, whatever is going on at the Palace?" The crowd asked.

The coat of arms above the door was bold and of gules. The hubbub reached the receiving hall where Dee was explaining. "The danger is crescive, her Majesty must be informed." Dee insisted. "She will be safe with an armed convoy at cock-shut-time."

The coat of arms above the door was bold and of red. The hubbub reached the receiving hall where Dee was explaining. "The danger is increasing, her Majesty must be informed." Dee insisted. "She will be safe with an armed escort at twilight, when cocks and hens go to roost."

The order came: "Coast the plan!"

The order came: "Advance the plan!"

"Such a plan is not eft," her Majesty began, following the man as he took the cranks in the Palace cellars to the secret hideaway.

"Such a plan is not convenient," her Majesty began, following the man as he took the winding passages in the Palace cellars to the secret hideaway.

The chant rose. "The Palace shall be convinced."

The chant rose. "The Palace shall be conquered."


He tripped on the path's coign, stumbled and caught himself. Hugging the wall cantle so as not to be seen as he approached the bourn, Hendrick hid behind a crumbled mure, listening.

He tripped on the path's projecting corner stone, stumbled and caught himself. Hugging the wall corner so as not to be seen as he approached the brook, Hendrick hid behind a crumbled wall, listening.

"Everything was in darraign, but I shall not be daffed." Hendrick said to himself. "I shall not drive."

"Everything was set in array, but I shall not be befooled." Hendrick said to himself. "I shall not rush impetuously."

He thought to himself: "This is a terrible hap to take." He shook his head. "I hope I will never be hight on it."

He thought to himself: "This is a terrible chance to take." He shook his head. "I hope I will never be called on it."

Then, he heard their leader speak. "When I give the imposition, you will leap into action without indurance."

Then, he heard their leader speak. "When I give the command, you will leap into action without delay."

Hendrick's eyes widened. He hadn't believed the plan until then.

Hendrick's eyes widened. He hadn't believed the plan until then.


"Who is here making inquistions?" Dee frowned.

"Who is here making enquiries?" Dee frowned.

"It is I, intending the Queen."

"It is I, regarding the Queen."

There was an intermission between the two men.

There was a pause between the two men.

"It is a trick. It is him who wishes her Majesty harm!" One man declared, pointing at Dee.

"It is a trick. It is him who wishes her Majesty harm!" One man declared, pointing at Dee.

Shaking his head, Dee sighed. "I would never and I do not weet the plan to take in the Palace."
Shaking his head, Dee sighed. "I would never and I do not know the plan to conquer the Palace."
"We will make him shrive." A Palace guard said.
"We will make him confess." A Palace guard said.
Dee muttered under his breath.
Dee muttered under his breath.

"He's using some kind of code. He's using castiliano vulgo." They exclaimed.
"He's using some kind of code. He's using discreet language." They exclaimed.
"Qualify your tone." Dee told him.
"Moderate your tone." Dee told him.
Silence fell.
Silence fell.

# 10.

"What betid?" The bellman asked.

"What happened?" The nightwatchman asked.

The tavern owner spoke. "They say he is nothing but an unbolted trojan, paying with a supposed stay!"

The tavern owner spoke. "They say he is nothing but an unrefined thief, paying with a counterfeit cheque!"

"He is a lifter." The other man shook his head, waving his cuttle at the accused.

"He is a thief." The other man shook his head, waving his knife at the accused.

"Sheath your cuttle or I shall have you set up for a shoulder-clapping." The bellman said.

"Sheath your knife or I shall have you set up for an arrest." The nightwatchman said.

The headborough took charge from the bellman, threatening the thief with engines and pilliwinks before the beak would send him to the derrick.

The arresting officer took charge from the nightwatchman, threatening the thief with instruments of torture and the torture device for pinching fingers before the magistrate would send him to the hangman.

"The charge is converyance. I will only need to attend quartan." The thief sneered.

"The charge is theft. I will only need to attend here every recurring four days." The thief sneered.

He received a slap around the head to quieten him.

He received a slap around the head to quieten him.

"Is there a meed?" The bellman was asked: he laughed.

"Is there a reward?" The nightwatchman was asked: he laughed.

## 11.

The group was operant here, that was obvious.
Hendrick hid when he saw three men approach.
The group was active here, that was obvious.
Hendrick hid when he saw three men approach.
"Contrary to belief, this is a mere cognizance." One
man said.
"Oppose to belief, this is a mere token." One man
said.
The instruction came then: "You must mammock
the stone."
The instruction came then: "You must break the
stone."
"That is offering." One man sighed.
"That is challenging." One man sighed.
"Frush it? We must fordo it." The first voice replied.
"Break it? We must destroy it." The first voice
replied.
It was be-moiled to hide it. Hendrick watched from
his hiding place.
It was daubed with dirt to hide it. Hendrick watched
from his hiding place.
"We must conster the truth. And not cozen." The
first man said.
"We must construe the truth. And not cheat." The
first man said.
"It will countervail." Another shook his head.
"It will counterpoise." Another shook his head.
"It is a matter of home urgency." The first man
urged. "There is no corollary. Do it!"

"It is a matter of the utmost urgency." The first man urged. "There is no surplus. Do it!"

Once the group had gone, Hendrick dug up the stone, seeing several symbols on it that he recognised. He knew then he had to take it to show Dr Dee and Katherine.

Once the group had gone, Hendrick dug up the stone, seeing several symbols on it that he recognised. He knew then he had to take it to show Dr Dee and Katherine.

## 12.

The farced head of a stag in one corner watched everyone in the room. They all wore chopin and a copatain hat, and a rabato. In Winter, their hats and gloves of cheveril kept them warm.

The stuffed head of a stag in one corner watched everyone in the room. They all wore high shoes and a high crowned hat, and a ruff. In Winter, their hats and gloves of kid leather kept them warm.

"It is your job to impress the guests." The blue-coat was told.

"It is your job to serve the guests." The servant was told.

A blue-coat stacked firing by the fireplace before shaking the napery over the table before the guests arrived for dinner.

A servant stacked firewood by the fireplace before shaking the table linen over the table before the guests arrived for dinner.

Serving the meal, he couldn't help but overhear the conversations.

Serving the meal, he couldn't help but overhear the conversations.

"There have been several grave occurents." The master of the house paused for effect. "The gardens are paled, for security."

"There have been several grave incidents." The master of the house paused for effect. "The gardens are fenced, for security."

The men shook their heads in disgust. "Amongst them, we must have mealed." One man shuddered.
The men shook their heads in disgust. "Amongst them, we must have mingled." One man shuddered.
Their meal passed pleasantly.
Their meal passed pleasantly.
"Have a biggen before you leave." They were bade.
"Have a night cap (drink) before you leave." They were bade.
Not one of them failed to enjoy the biggen, he saw.
Not one of them failed to enjoy the night cap, he saw.

# 13.

In Dee's lab, Hendrick laid the stone on the table for him and Katherine to examine: they took it to another room.

In Dee's lab, Hendrick laid the stone on the table for him and Katherine to examine: they took it to another room.

It was then he saw the papers on time travel and wormholes although he did not understand them. They were half under the working that Dr Dee called a calendar. It was another great work that Hendrick did not understand.

It was then he saw the papers on time travel and wormholes, although he did not understand them. They were half under the working that Dr Dee called a calendar. It was another great work that Hendrick did not understand.

When Dr Dee returns, he is reading the papers.

When Dr Dee returns, he is reading the papers.

"You are a braid, motley-minded mome." Dee told him, mistempered.

"You are a deceitful, foolish stupid person." Dee told him, angry.

Hendrick's expression was wailful and he was afeared. "I am sorriest for my gain-givings."

Hendrick's expression was lamentable and he was afraid. "I am most sorrowful for my misgivings."

Mammering, Dee accepts his apology.

Hesitating, Dee accepts his apology.

"I want to learn more." Hendrick whispered.

"I want to learn more." Hendrick whispered.

Dee showed him extracts in his diary then, telling tales of hardiment from lands far away.

Dee showed him extracts in his diary then, telling tales of defiance and brave deeds from lands far away.

"My stay with the geographer, Gerardus Mercator, was more than a fleet. He produced an atlas, a book with maps from all over the world. Such a complement."

"My stay with the geographer, Gerardus Mercator, was more than a way to pass the time. He produced an atlas, a book with maps from all over the world. Such an accomplishment."

Hendrick nodded.

Hendrick nodded.

"He gave me a largess of the latten staff and globes." Dee pointed to the items.

"He gave me a present of the brass staff and globes." Dee pointed to the items.

"The communication crystal from Uriel the angel is a gaze." Hendrick said then.

"The communication crystal from Uriel the angel is an object of wonder." Hendrick said then.

Dee nodded wisely.

Dee nodded wisely.

"After the occurents of a new star and a comet, my know helped Queen Elizabeth to build a great Navy under Drake. They had quiddits and promptures, but were prone to capitulate."

"After the incidents of a new star and a comet, my knowledge helped Queen Elizabeth to build a great Navy under Drake. They had subtle questions and suggestions but were willing to work together."

"What other complements have you made?" Hendrick asked after a while.

"What other accomplishments have you made?" Hendrick asked after a while.

Dee smiled. "I agreed to holp James Burbage in the building of the Theatre. After his lethe, his sons had to cog the building anight and rebuilt it as the Globe in Southwark."

Dee smiled. "I agreed to help James Burbage in the building of the Theatre. After his death, his sons had to dissemble the building by night and rebuilt it as the Globe in Southwark."

Hendrick's mouth dropped open in shock.

Hendrick's mouth dropped open in shock.

"In the future, there will be no need for a wherry, there will be a tunnel under the Thames." Dee told him, smiling at his shock. "I can prenominate the future."

"In the future, there will be no need for a small boat used for river crossings, there will be a tunnel under the Thames." Dee told him, smiling at his shock. "I can name beforehand the future."

"What else will happen in the future?" Hendrick asked.

"What else will happen in the future?" Hendrick asked.

"Many importing finds." Dee said.

*145*

"Many significant finds." Dee said.

"And?"

"And?"

"The palabras of the metaphysical will be festinately forbode." Dee shook his head.

"The words of the supernatural will be quickly forbidden." Dee shook his head.

A thought struck Hendrick. "Will you be able to travel to the future?"

A thought struck Hendrick. "Will you be able to travel to the future?"

Dee nodded wisely.

Dee nodded wisely.

Hendrick stared at him agazed.

Hendrick stared at him in amazement.

# Books by Yvonne Marrs

Introduction to the Fictional Work of Yvonne Marrs

When The Sax Man Plays Part 1 - Making It

When The Sax Man Plays Part 2 - Proving It

When The Sax Man Plays Part 3 - Managing It

When The Sax Man Plays Part 4 - His Return

When The Sax Man Plays Part 5 - The Prequel

When The Sax Man Plays ...and All That Jazz

Football Crazy 1: A World Cup Adventure

Football Crazy 2: On The Edge of Glory

Football Crazy 3: The Hat-trick

Football Crazy 4: A Point to Prove

Football Crazy 5: The Master of Managerial Psychology

Aiden Lewis Octet Book 1 - Memoirs

Aiden Lewis Octet Book 2 - Reminiscence

Aiden Lewis Octet Book 3 - Touring

Aiden Lewis Octet Book 4 - Bravado

Aiden Lewis Octet Book 5 - Partnership

Aiden Lewis Octet Book 6 - Vulnerable

Aiden Lewis Octet Book 7 - Struggles

Aiden Lewis Octet Book 8 - Denouement

Undeserved 1

Undeserved 2

Undeserved 3

Putting The Visible Into So-Called Invisible
Illnesses Through Poetry

Castiliano Vulgo - An Elizabethan Story

Harbourtown Murder

Inexorable

Termination at the Halt

Can't Buy Health 1

Can't Buy Health 2

Can't Buy Health 3

Can't Buy Health 4

Can't Buy Health 5

Can't Buy Health 6

Can't Buy Health 7

Can't Buy Health 8

We hope you have enjoyed this book, please leave a review for Yvonne.

Printed in Great Britain
by Amazon

21751237R00086